Dawson: He's ~~wondering~~ what went wrong. So it couldn't hurt for him to be around Joey for a long weekend. Could it?

Joey: She's ready to risk making a fool of herself as a beginner on the slopes. Now two ski hunks are making fools of themselves over her.

Pacey: Well, well, well. A ski chalet with a hot tub. Now he just needs to find a friend to share the wealth with him . . .

Jen: She didn't expect Dawson to add Joey to the invitation. But now that Joey's no longer interested in Dawson, is it Jen's chance to spend some time together with him?

DAWSON'S CREEK™

Dawson's Creek™

Major Meltdown

Based on the television series "Dawson's Creek™"
created by **Kevin Williamson**

Written by K. S. Rodriguez

POCKET BOOKS
New York   London   Toronto   Sydney   Tokyo   Singapore

8766305

An *Original* Publication of POCKET BOOKS

POCKET BOOKS, a division of Simon & Schuster Inc.
1230 Avenue of the Americas, New York, NY 10020

ISBN: 0-671-02477-9

First Pocket Books printing January 1999

10 9 8 7 6 5 4 3 2 1

POCKET and colophon are registered trademarks of Simon & Schuster Inc.

DAWSON'S CREEK is a registered trademark of Columbia TriStar Television, Inc.

Printed in the U.S.A.

For Creek Fans Lisa Grant, Suzanne Flenard, and Alexandra Peredo

Special Thanks to Ingrid van der Leeden, Rodger Weinfeld, and everyone at Pocket Books

Major Meltdown

Chapter 1

"**B**rrr! It's like the Antarctic out there," Dawson Leery said as he stepped into the S.S. Ice House and slammed the door shut. He stamped his wet, booted feet by the door and shivered before he spotted his friends, Pacey Witter and Jen Lindley, waving him over to their table. It was easy to find them; the restaurant was empty on this freezing, wet, late Monday afternoon.

"The iceman cometh," Pacey cracked when Dawson approached their table. "You look like you were just discovered by archaeologists and thawed out from an iceberg."

Jen smiled, putting down her menu. "He's right. Did you swim over here or what?"

"Practically," Dawson said as he sat down. "I can't wait until I get my license so I don't have to walk everywhere."

"Can you say raincoat? How about umbrella? Repeat after me," Joey Potter chimed in as she swung by their table. "Um-brel-la."

"Hey, Joe," Dawson said in what he hoped was a nonchalant tone, as he pulled off his drenched ski jacket. Usually he could take her chiding, but today it just annoyed him. Joey looked so beautiful and . . . dry . . . and . . . unobtainable in her chartreuse turtleneck and work apron. It seemed that every time he willed himself to get over her, he started to miss her all over again.

Not that he didn't see her all the time. They were still friends. But things were different now, not like they used to be. The days of easy teasing, comfortable conversations, or her spending the night platonically in his bedroom were over. All of that changed when they started to get involved. And now that they weren't together anymore, it was hard to go backward and resume their lifelong friendship like nothing had happened.

"What does one have to do to get served around here?" Dawson asked the room in general.

"Hey!" Joey said. "I wouldn't try that tone of voice on the staff if I were you."

Dawson slung his jacket on the back of an extra chair, in the process sending drops of water flying.

Joey jumped back. "That's it—special sauce for you!" she said, her tone half-annoyed, half-kidding.

Dawson smiled a tight smile. "I'm hungry. Anyone want to split some fries?" He cocked an eyebrow in Pacey and Jen's direction.

"Um—" Pacey said uncomfortably, tugging at the collar of his unseasonable bowling shirt. "I think I'll get my own . . ."

Dawson laughed. "You don't think she's serious—about the special sauce stuff, do you?"

"Well . . ." Pacey started, shooting Joey a cagey look.

"I wouldn't worry about it, Pacey," Joey said as she pulled out her pad from her apron. "It's never bothered you before. I think you actually like the 'special sauce.' "

Pacey's eyes widened in horror, while Dawson and Jen burst out laughing.

"Why . . . what . . . what did I ever do?" Pacey stammered.

"You exist. Your mere, vile presence automatically qualifies you for the chef's special. The chef, by the way, has a nasty flu bug today," Joey answered, deadpan. Then she poised her pen over the pad, and asked cheerfully, "Now, what would you guys like to order?"

"Cheeseburger, fries, the usual," Dawson said.

"I'll have the chicken fingers," Jen added. "With honey mustard—no barbecue, please."

Joey scribbled down their orders. "Okay. Pacey?" she asked politely. "What can I get you on this fine winter afternoon?"

Pacey threw his menu down on the wooden table. "Nothing, thank you," he said tersely. "I don't seem to be hungry anymore. I lost my appetite."

"Oh," Joey said in mock surprise. "Too bad." She turned toward the kitchen. "I'll go wake up the cook now." she muttered as she walked away.

"I don't know why I even bother coming here," Pacey grumbled.

"She was just kidding," Dawson said. "Lighten up."

"I wouldn't put it past her," Pacey insisted, furrowing his brow. "Think about what goes on in the mind of a screwed-up, sexually repressed, misanthropic, maladjusted chick in charge of food. The possibilities are endless . . . and quite frightening, my friend."

Dawson shook his head and chuckled again. Pacey always managed to make him laugh—even when he was wet, grumpy, and cold.

But Pacey wasn't laughing at all, Dawson noticed. If possible, he was even moodier than Dawson these days. "All this freezing rain is depressing me," Pacey said, changing the subject. "When is it going to snow?"

"Yeah," Jen agreed. "I think the rain is giving us all the winter blahs." She twirled a lock of blonde hair around her finger. "I never used to get them back home in New York," she added.

"No," Pacey quipped. "There, you just got tuberculosis from the rats in the streets. But never the winter blahs."

"Very funny," Jen shot back. "I just miss winter in New York. There's nothing like walking down a tree-lined street in the Village, just to see the new-fallen snow on the iron banisters and stoops of every townhouse. Or the skaters in Rockefeller Center, with the gigantic lighted tree looming up behind them. It's like a wonderland," she went on nostalgically. "And nothing ever shuts down. Even when there is a snowstorm, you could walk to a local restaurant, and it would be full of people, chattering about the weather in good spirits. Or you could go to the movies, or rent a video—"

"Or go to school, since you barely have snow days," Pacey finished. "Or go to work after school, and walk there in the miserable, freezing storm since there won't be any cabs available. Or you could take the subway, where eight million people will cough twice as many diseases on you in tight quarters."

"All right already, you made your point, beach bum. You really *are* in a mood today," Jen said defensively. "What's your problem, anyway?"

"My problem? My problem is that yet another winter is going to go by where I have no one to warm up my bones," Pacey snapped. "And no offense, Jen, but the girls in Capeside are growing awfully tiresome. That's my problem."

Realization dawned on Jen. "Just where *is* Andie, anyway?" she said.

Pacey shrugged. "Don't look at me. Andie asked for space—so I'm giving it to her."

Joey passed by, carrying a tray. "Food will be up in a sec," she said. "And Andie and Jack went to Providence with their mom to visit their dad."

"I hear what you're saying," Dawson said to Pacey. "We need a change of personnel on this movie set, that's for sure. I could stand to meet some new girls." And he did want a change of scenery where the female persuasion was concerned. Sitting right next to him was Jen, the first girl in Capeside to dump him. Waiting on their table was Joey, dumper number two. Maybe it was time to check out another town . . .

That gave Dawson an idea. "We have a long weekend because of President's Day. Why don't we go on another road trip?" he suggested, his hopes high for better luck than they had on their past adventure in New York. He did get lucky and met a fabulous girl in Providence when he was glum after Jen dumped him. But he wanted to go somewhere else. Somewhere wintry and snowy. "What about Vermont? We could go skiing!"

"That's a great idea," Pacey said. "If you're Donald Trump. Do you have any idea how much it costs to get a place to stay on a holiday weekend? Too much, that's how much. Especially last minute."

"Yeah," Dawson agreed glumly, all visions of mountaintop romance dissolving. "I guess you're right. I don't even have enough saved from the video store for gas to get there."

"I love Vermont," Jen said wistfully. "It's so cozy and fun. We used to go up every year to our cab—" Her face suddenly lit up. "Hey! My parents have a cabin in Steep Mountain! They hardly ever use it anymore," she said excitedly. "In fact, they're going to be away this weekend . . ."

Dawson and Pacey hung on to her every word. "Did you say cabin? In Steep Mountain?" Pacey repeated.

"Sure did," Jen said happily. "I can't think of a better way to get rid of the winter blahs than skiing. What do you guys say?"

"I'm in," Pacey said, perking up for the first time all afternoon. "I can even drive—"

Dawson held up his hands. "Whoa! Wait a minute. I don't know if I want to subject myself to two and a half hours of Mr. Toad's Wild Ride—especially in the ice and snow," he said.

"Hey, it's all legal now. Or did you forget that I

finally passed my driver's test?" Pacey said proudly. "I am officially licensed by the state of Massachusetts, which is more than I can say for you, chump. Unless you feel like hitchhiking, I'm it."

"Good point," Dawson said, backing down. "I guess I'm willing to risk it. As long as we get out of here."

"Risk what? Going where?" Joey asked as she set down a tray full of food. She placed a cheeseburger and fries in front of Dawson, and the chicken fingers in front of Jen.

Dawson dove into his food right away as Pacey eyed the goods warily. "Mmmm, good sauce today!" Dawson teased with his mouth full. "Next time I plan on being extra obnoxious. Such flavor!"

Joey laughed and searched the empty restaurant. Not a customer was in sight. She grabbed a seat and sat at the end of the table. "Really—where are you guys going? Somewhere fun?" she asked again.

That's when it hit Dawson—the freshly fallen snow. A roaring fire. Maybe even a horse-drawn sleighride. Vermont in winter was definitely one of the most romantic places he knew. Maybe instead of meeting new girls, whose intimacies he couldn't count on after a whirlwind weekend, he could re-spark a little romance with Joey and win back the girl of his dreams. After all, he'd never seen that girl in Providence again, though they'd e-mailed each other. What was the point, when he could be with Joey.

"We're going to go skiing this weekend," Dawson explained. "Jen's parents have a cabin in Steep Mountain—so we can stay for free. Can you come?"

Joey raised her eyebrows in interest. "Steep Mountain? Sounds fun . . . but I have to work this weekend."

"That's too bad," Jen said quickly, as Pacey shot her a skeptical look. "It would have been fun for all of us to be there."

"But it's so slow," Dawson cut in. "You sure that Bessie couldn't give you the weekend off? With us gone you won't have any customers at all."

"I don't really know how to ski, but I always meant to learn . . ." Joey continued thoughtfully.

"It's a great place to learn!" Dawson said eagerly. "There's a bunny hill there for beginners—right, Jen?"

"Right," Jen answered, not too enthusiastically.

"Well . . . I guess there's no harm in asking for time off," Joey said. She rose from the table in search of her sister. "I'll be right back."

When Joey walked away, Pacey glared at Dawson. "I knew it," he said, shaking his head.

"Knew what?" Dawson asked. What was Pacey's problem all of a sudden? He found it hard to keep up with his moods. One minute, he was psyched about Dawson's idea to go skiing. The next minute, he seemed angry with him.

"What happened to 'change of scenery'? What happened to meeting new girls? I knew you would lame out on the babe hunt, just to moon over your old *friend*," Pacey accused. "Or did you suddenly forget why we were in desperate need of a road trip?"

Dawson gasped in protest. "I am not mooning over her," he said indignantly, though he privately

8

knew Pacey was right. "I was merely including her. We're all friends, right?"

"Right," Jen said flatly, sticking a chicken finger in her mouth.

"Oh, yeah," Pacey said mockingly. "Best buds. Now I *know* I'm going to be stuck ski-bunny hunting alone. While you're making 'friends.'"

Their conversation reached an abrupt halt when Joey trotted back to the table. "Guess what?" she said excitedly. "I can have off! I can go!"

"Great!" Dawson said enthusiastically, pushing aside all of Pacey's remarks. He could picture it now: Joey wobbling helplessly on her skis, falling right into Dawson's capable arms.

And so what if Pacey was right. He had to take every chance he could get. Pacey just didn't understand, Dawson mused.

"Okay, see you later," Jen said to Joey as she walked out of the Icehouse and got into Pacey's father's truck with Dawson.

"Crank up the heat!" a shivering Dawson said between chattering teeth.

"All right," Pacey said, as he threw the gear into reverse. The truck lurched backward, and Pacey slammed on the brakes.

"Pacey!" Jen complained as she was jolted right onto Dawson's lap.

"There's no way," Dawson groaned, "that I'm going to be able to take this all the way to Vermont. Can't you drive like a human being?"

Jen laughed and smiled up at Dawson before she straightened herself up from his lap. It felt good to be this close to him again, Jen thought. It had taken so long for things to get back to normal with him after their breakup.

As Pacey put the truck in forward, then eased out of the parking lot, Jen admired Dawson's profile. He was certainly handsome. She liked the way his dirty blond hair framed his face. She adored the way the purposeful dark lines of his eyebrows accentuated his thoughtful brown eyes. She especially loved his down-to-earth friendly smile, that brought out the innocent little boy in him. She cherished those moments when he could turn from soft to intense in a split second, like when he talked about his filmmaking.

Dawson had no idea what hunk potential he had. That's what made him stand apart from all of the other puffed-up vanity cases she'd dated before him.

She looked away so Dawson wouldn't notice her staring. She missed him. They were great friends, but lately she missed the way he'd tail after her in the school hallway, like a puppy-dog, and she longed for the days when he'd dawdle at her back porch after a date. Most of all, she pined for his tender touch, and soft, lingering kisses. She loved how he was so full of desire, but always a gentleman.

Her love life had been one big bore lately. No one doted on her like Dawson once did. She wondered if anyone would ever again. Many times, she wondered if she had made a mistake by letting Dawson go.

That's why she, like Pacey, wasn't overly excited about Joey joining them on the trip. She hadn't planned on excluding Joey, but Jen was sure that she'd be working. While Pacey ventured out in search of a new breed of girls, Jen was hoping that Dawson would rediscover her, in the privacy of a steaming hot tub, perhaps, or at a cozy inn, over a candlelight dinner.

Jen sighed. It wasn't going to happen. He'd be puppy-dogging behind Joey all weekend long. She just had to try her best to deal with it, and enjoy herself nonetheless.

"We should leave as soon as we can after school on Friday," Jen pointed out, trying to take her mind off what might or might not happen over the weekend. "There will be a lot of holiday traffic. Especially the direction we're going."

"No prob," Pacey said.

"I'll pack all my stuff and bring it to school," Dawson added.

"Me, too," Pacey agreed.

Within minutes Pacey pulled up to Jen's driveway. She dreaded opening the door and escaping the warm comfort of the truck, no matter how Pacey drove. Bracing herself, she pulled open the car door. A stream of hail pounded her on the face.

Jen pulled her hood up tightly and stepped out of the car, Dawson following behind her. "Thanks, man," Dawson called.

"Ditto," Jen shouted, as Pacey raced away, the clunky truck fishtailing on the road.

Dawson quickly turned to Jen before he trotted next door to his house. "See you tomorrow," he said.

"Bye," she called, as she ran toward the front door, wishing that Dawson had given her one of his bone-crushing hugs or soft mushy kisses before he went inside.

But the icy rain on Jen's face snapped her out of her daydreams. Quickly, she raced up her porch, careful not to slip and fall on the slick stairs.

She pulled open her front door and felt a wave of heat envelop her body. "Grams!" she called out. "I'm home."

Lately, since Jen's social life had been so poor, Grams didn't have the occasion to peek out the window at her when she came home. Sadly, Grams knew that Jen was perfectly safe with Dawson these days.

How pathetic, Jen thought. But while Grams was loosening up in some ways, and she and Jen had grown closer since Gramps died, she was still incredibly old-fashioned and overprotective in plenty of other ways.

That's when it hit her. Jen drew in a short breath of panic.

Grams.

Jen completely forgot about her and didn't factor her into the equation of the weekend.

How was she ever going to get permission from Grams to go away for the weekend alone with friends?

Chapter 2

"Well, well, well," Doug Witter said as soon as Pacey stepped in the front door. "You actually have the courage to show your face in the Witter household, after what you pulled this afternoon."

Pacey took off his coat, and unlaced his soaking hiking boots. Pacey hated when his brother got on his authority trip. He was wearing the smirk that Pacey hated; the smirk that said, "Ha, ha, ha, you screwed up again."

"What?" Pacey asked defensively. "What'd I do now?"

"Dad needed the truck this afternoon," Doug said over his shoulder, as he strolled into the family room and flopped on the couch. Pacey followed on his heels. "But for some unknown reason, it wasn't here," Doug went on. He put on his best mock-innocent expression. "Do you have any idea what might have happened?"

13

"Didn't he get the note I left him after school?" Pacey asked. "I left him a note telling him that I'd just be using it for a couple of hours."

Doug looked at Pacey, feigning confusion. "Hmmm . . . a note, a note," he said, as he picked up the remote control and started to absentmindedly flip through channels. Pacey hated when he did that. He couldn't leave one channel on for more than five seconds.

"Hmmm . . . wait a minute!" Doug continued, making a show of scratching his chin in thought. "That wouldn't have been the piece of paper I found in the kitchen and put my gum in, would it?"

Pacey instantly filled with rage. Why did Doug have to sabotage everything he did? He just didn't understand what kind of a sick thrill his older brother got out of constantly getting him in trouble.

"You know," Pacey spat, "I'd think that someone in his mid-twenties would have better things to do than to screw up my life." He clenched his fists, holding back every impulse to punch Doug's lights out. "I just wish that Capeside would open an all-male nude review to give you something else to do besides pick on me!"

"Or maybe Capeside should open a dweeb colony, so we could put dateless rejects like you there," Doug shot back.

That was it. Doug had touched Pacey's sore spot, and Pacey wasn't going to stand for it anymore. He dove at Doug, pinning him to the couch. Pacey lifted his fist to pop him right in the mouth, but Doug was faster and stronger. He grabbed Pacey's fist and held on to it, just as a shout boomed throughout the room.

"Pacey! What are you doing?" It was Sheriff Witter, and he didn't sound too happy.

"He asked for it!" Pacey said, jumping off the couch.

"I was just minding my own business watching TV," Doug said innocently, "when psycho-boy just leaped at me for no reason."

"That's not true!" Pacey shouted.

"Have you considered getting him psychological help, Dad? Or can't we send him to some kind of home for mentally unbalanced, wayward boys?" Doug asked, making Pacey even angrier.

"Enough!" Mr. Witter hollered. "Pacey—go to your room. I'm tired of your behavior and your thoughtlessness. I thought someone had stolen the truck this afternoon!"

Pacey grumbled as he stalked past his dad down the hall and up the stairs. It was so unfair. His dad was always on his case and never had a bad word for precious deputy Doug. He wondered how he ended up with this family from another planet.

Or maybe *he* was the one from another planet. How in the world did he, Pacey Witter, end up the son of a sheriff and the youngest of five siblings? How in the world did he end up with three preoccupied sisters who barely knew he existed and a brother from hell, who had an inexplicable vendetta against him?

"And your car privileges are revoked," Mr. Witter bellowed from the bottom of the stairs. "Understand?"

"Perfectly," Pacey groused before he slammed his door shut.

He flopped onto his bed. Perfect, just perfect. Now how in the world were they going to get to Vermont this weekend?

Car or no car, Pacey was determined to get out of the Witter House of Horrors. No matter what, he'd find a way. And maybe, just maybe, he would never come back.

Jen sat in the windowseat, curled up with a book. She kept reading the same paragraph over and over again, because she couldn't concentrate. Putting the book down, she glanced out the window at the pounding hail outside. The porch light illuminated the storm, making it appear as if the stars were falling outside.

Jen could hear Grams bustling around in the kitchen, fixing dinner. She had to spring the Vermont trip on her, but how?

What was she going to say? A dozen schemes crowded her mind. Maybe Jen should say that she was joining the debate team, and they had a match in Vermont. But were they even called matches? She didn't know. Perhaps she should choose something with which she was more familiar.

A club . . . She could say she joined the ski club, and their first outing was going to be in Vermont. Jen held her chin thoughtfully. That might work, she reasoned. She could come up with a phony permission slip by Friday. But already Jen could hear the countless questions and information Grams would require: Who was the chaperone? Where would you be staying? How can I reach you in case of emergency? She would have to tell too many lies. No good.

She could say that she was going to see her parents for the weekend . . . Jen nixed that idea as soon as she thought it up. Her mom spoke to Grams way too often. She'd be busted in the blink of an eye.

But she liked the idea of involving her parents. It gave her an idea. Her parents had been feeling incredibly guilty since they'd sent her up to Capeside to live. And they've been getting good reports from Grams.

What if she appealed to a higher authority than Grams? Jen smiled at her reflection in the frosty window pane. It was a great idea: a win-win situation. She could probably guilt her parents into letting her go. And she wouldn't have to lie and scheme to Grams.

It was the perfect plan. Now all she had to do was get in touch with the good old 'rents.

Jen got up from the windowseat and grabbed the phone receiver off the wall. She carefully dialed her parents' number, praying that they would be home. When were they going away, anyway? she wondered as the phone rang. She sure hoped they weren't gone yet—then she would be sunk.

"Daddy!" she nearly shrieked when her father picked up the phone. She was prepared to play Daddy's little girl to the hilt.

"How are you sweetheart?" Dad responded in his usual, formal tone.

"I'm doing great. I wanted to speak to you and

Mom before you left for London. When are you leaving?"

"Wednesday," her father responded. "But your Mom's not in right now. Salon night, remember?"

"Right," Jen said. She had to admit she was a little relieved that Mom wasn't around. If she got her dad's permission, Grams wouldn't challenge it. But if it were her Mom, Grams would no doubt grab the phone and say something like, "Are you sure that's a good idea?"

"So, when are you coming back?" Jen asked, then added for good guilt measure, "When am I going to see you again?"

"Next Wednesday," he replied. "Then when work slows down we'll pop up to visit you in Capeside, darling, I promise. How are things up there?"

"The weather is terrible. I miss you, Daddy," Jen said, a pout in her voice. "And New York in the winter. It's so rainy and cold here . . ."

"Well, you're not missing anything here, sweetheart. It's pretty much the same story in New York—mostly miserable. I don't think we're going to get any snow this season."

Now's the time, Jen thought. Go for it. "I miss the snow. I was thinking of all the great times we used to have in the Steep Mountain cabin. We haven't been there in so long."

"Yes," her father answered a little sadly. "I'm sorry we haven't been able to spend time together as a family . . ." His voice trailed off.

Jen knew she had him right where she wanted him. "Well, I was wondering," she ventured. "I

18

mean, I'm so close here, and it's President's Day weekend coming up. Would I be able to use the cabin this weekend? Maybe see the snow and go skiing with some friends?"

"Sure, sweetheart," he said, but added tentatively, "it should be all free and clear. Just as long as you don't wreck the place."

"Oh, don't worry," Jen assured him. "It would just be me, my friend Josephine," she used Joey's real name so her father wouldn't think she was going with three boys, "and the boy next door, Dawson, and Pacey Witter."

"Sounds fine, darling," her father said. "You know where we leave the key."

"Thanks, Dad!" Jen said. "You're the greatest!"

"Anything for you, sweetheart," her father responded. "How's your grandmother? Is she around?"

Perfect! Jen thought. Now *he* could spring it on her! "I'll get her, Dad." She called out to Grams, then quickly added, "I haven't had a chance to tell her about my plans yet . . ."

"I'll fill her in," her father offered, just as she hoped.

She heard the click of Grams picking up the other extension, and she said a fond goodbye to her father before she placed the receiver back in its cradle.

Everything had worked beautifully. Now she was home free—ready for a three-day weekend full of snow, skiing, fun, and hopefully a little romance.

Adults, she mused, as she picked up her book

and resumed her post in the windowseat. They were so easy to manipulate.

Dawson sat in his room watching a clip from a short film he had made. He rewound it when Joey appeared on the screen, tossing her hair dramatically as she looked woefully out across the creek.

He stopped the tape. This film was made in their better days, when Dawson fantasized about being a famous director, with Joey his leading lady, on and off the screen, beside him.

Those days were over, he thought dismally. He hadn't been able to make a new film lately. The awful weather, and his miserable love life had sucked his creative energy dry.

He popped out the tape, and took out a notebook to brainstorm story ideas for a film in the spring. He was determined to get past this block; he wouldn't let the weather—or Joey—keep him down for long.

He heard the telephone ring, and then his father's distinct call from downstairs. "Dawson! Phone!" Dawson threw down his pen. It was no use. Whenever he set his mind to creating, something interrupted him.

It was probably almost dinner time, anyway, he realized, so he trotted down the stairs to take the cordless from his father's hand.

"Pacey," his father said, handing it over.

"Thanks," Dawson said to his father. "What's up?" he asked into the receiver.

"Nothing is up, man," Pacey said hopelessly. "Everything is one huge, gigantic, downer."

"Wow," Dawson said, laughing. "You are really the king of gloom and doom today. What's the matter now?"

"Besides the usual stuff, Dad took away my car privileges," Pacey told Dawson. "No wheels! Do you know what that means?"

"You have to walk to school?" Dawson asked, missing the point. He walked into the kitchen and opened the refrigerator, cradling the phone in his neck.

"No! It means we have no way to get to Vermont!" Pacey shouted, exasperated. "But I don't care if we have to take a bus. We're going. I have to get out of here. My Stepford family is driving me stark-raving mad!"

"Okay," Dawson said, pouring himself some soda. "Calm down. Maybe we can work something out. Maybe my dad will let me take a car for the weekend. They have two, after all."

"That would be more than awesome," Pacey said, brightening up. "Do you think your dad will go for it?"

"I don't know, but I can try," Dawson said quietly into the phone, aware that his dad might be in earshot. "But you have to promise to be very, very careful driving. Okay?"

"I promise," Pacey swore. "I'll drive however you want—like an old lady—whatever it takes to get me out of the general vicinity of my family and girls who know better than to date me."

"Okay," Dawson said. "I'll call you back."

Dawson hung up the phone and hesitated before going to his dad. He didn't know how his dad would feel about Pacey driving his car for the weekend. *If only I had my license,* Dawson thought, for what seemed like the umpteenth time that day. It seemed like his sixteenth birthday would take an eternity to arrive.

He knew that in these situations, strategy was everything. Putting on his gloomiest expression, Dawson trudged into the TV room and sat down next to his dad, who was intently reading a newspaper.

Dawson let out a huge sigh.

Mr. Leery peered over the top of his newspaper over at Dawson. "What's the matter, son?" he asked.

"Oh," Dawson said sadly. "It's just that all of our plans that I just told you about for the weekend are ruined."

"You mean the ski trip?" his father asked curiously, putting the paper down. "Why? What happened?"

Dawson sighed again. "Pacey's dad. He isn't very generous with lending his car," Dawson said, inwardly admiring the way he was handling his dad, setting him up to save the day. "And since he's the only licensed driver, we're sunk." A brand-new idea struck him. "Unless we could rent a car . . ." he added.

"I'm afraid you can't," Mr. Leery told him. "I think you have to be twenty-five to rent a car in Massachusetts."

"Oh," Dawson said, deflated. "I guess that means our plans are really ruined."

"What about Jen or Joey? Do they have access to a car?" Mr. Leery asked.

Dawson shook his head. "No. Bessie needs her truck. And Jen's grandmother only has one car, too." He hesitated. "And I don't envision her as a car-lending type, if you know what I mean."

"Well," Mr. Leery said thoughtfully. "That's a shame. Sorry kiddo," he said, then went back to reading his paper.

Dawson's heart sunk. He had to press. But how? Should he just out-and-out ask? He decided to try one more tactic, which was usually fail proof. "Yeah. It seems like I'm the only kid in Capeside with generous, giving parents," he hedged.

Mr. Leery put down his paper again. "Boy, you can really lay it on thick, when you need to," he said, not taken in by Dawson's flattery. "If it were you driving, I'd have no problem lending the car. It's just that I don't know about someone else— Pacey—driving it . . ."

"Oh, Pacey's an excellent driver!" Dawson piped up. "Really, dad! He's the safest driver I know."

Mr. Leery shot his son a skeptical look. "Wasn't there a drama around here not too long ago about him failing his driver's test?"

"Oh, that," Dawson said, waving his hand. "He only missed by one question." Dawson hated to lie to his dad, but this was too important to him. "When he took the test again he passed with flying colors. Honest." At least that part was true.

Mr. Leery cocked a suspicious eyebrow at Dawson.

Dawson knew he had no choice but to get real with his dad. "Listen, Dad," he pleaded. "I would hold you in the highest esteem—as the coolest Dad

23

in the world—if you would just lend us your car. I swear, we'll be so careful. It's just that I'm really looking forward to this trip. And I was hoping to spend some time with Joey . . ."

"Say no more," Mr. Leery cut in. "I won't stand in the way of true romance. You can have the car. But you are fully responsible for anything that might happen," he added firmly.

Dawson leaped up from the couch. "Thanks, Dad!" he bellowed. "You're the best!"

As he sped out of the family room to call Pacey back, Dawson gave his father the thumbs up. His "false flattery" was all true, he knew. His Dad was generous, giving, and above all, understanding. Dawson knew he was awfully lucky to have him.

Now he just hoped this weekend he would be as lucky in love as he was in lineage.

Chapter 3

"**W**ow, Dawson, has your father taken up drinking or something?" Joey asked incredulously as she followed Jen into the backseat of the Leery car.

"No," Dawson answered, craning his neck around from the front seat. "Why do you ask that?"

"I just can't believe he's allowing Capeside's own village idiot to drive his car for the weekend, that's all," she said, nodding at Pacey in the driver's seat.

Pacey turned around and glared at Joey impatiently. "Backseat unlicensed drivers offering unsolicited driving comments, jokes, or advice will not be tolerated in this vehicle."

"All right," Joey said. "Just show me where the seat belt is. And are you sure those air bags work, Dawson?"

"It's nice of Pacey to drive us," Jen said, getting

up off Joey's seat belt on which she was sitting. "I don't think we should give him a hard time."

"Thank you," Pacey said pointedly, as he started the ignition.

"Until at least after we get there," Jen added good-naturedly.

Pacey ignored her and pulled out of the school parking lot. He veered onto Main Street and let out a whoop. "We're free!" he yelled. "We are on our way!"

While Pacey slid the car out onto the highway, Joey sat back and relaxed. It was going to be a fun weekend, no doubt. She had always wanted to learn to be a good skier, but she had never had the money to go. She'd saved up a lot from the summer season at the Ice House last year, most of which was put aside for college. But once in a while, Joey allowed herself to splurge, and since they had a place to stay, she figured, why not take advantage of it.

Plus, Joey had good memories associated with one time she had gone skiing, when she was a little girl. Her mother had taken her and Bessie to a local bunny hill, and Joey had the time of her life. She remembered laughing when she fell, while other kids were crying. She recalled wondering what there was to cry about. Falling in the snow was fun!

She chuckled to herself at the memory of Bessie crashing into the ski instructor, knocking the woman over. She also remembered Mom waving proudly from the sidelines, giggling with delight.

But that was a long time ago.

Now that she was older, Joey reasoned that falling probably wasn't as much fun anymore. She certainly couldn't afford to break any bones. She suddenly had a bout of insecurity about the whole thing. She really didn't remember how to ski; just the good time she had with Mom and Bessie. She didn't know the first thing to do. "I hope I'm able to stand up on the skis," she remarked.

"You should do fine," Jen promised. "In the paper this morning the ski report said that conditions are great in Vermont—all powder. It's much easier for beginners when it's not icy."

Dawson shifted in his seat so he faced the girls in the back. "I'll be happy to give you lessons," he offered eagerly.

That's exactly what Joey was afraid of. No offense to Dawson, but she didn't want to spend too much time alone with him. It just made room for misunderstandings—and she didn't want to get his hopes up about getting back together.

"Thanks for the offer," she said, "but the resort gives a free sample lesson."

Joey brandished the page she had torn out of a skiing magazine.

Dawson's expression turned from eager to disappointed. "But my lessons are free, too," he pressed.

He wasn't taking the hint, Joey figured, or he was just a masochist who wanted to be told to bug off. Joey fought her impulses and said politely, "Nah. It wouldn't be fun for you to spend the whole day stuck on the bunny hill. I'd feel guilty."

Dawson turned back around in his seat. Joey could tell that he was wounded. "Okay, then," he said.

Joey loved Dawson in so many ways. But their

relationship was intense enough as it was. Taking it farther was cause for psychological meltdown. She was enjoying her freedom from all of the emotional ups and downs. She just wished that Dawson would do the same.

She leaned her head against the car window. As they zoomed down the interstate, she watched droplets of rain change to puffy white flakes of snow. They grew heavier, came down more quickly, but tumbled gracefully to the ground, like heavenly ballerinas in frilly white tutus spinning out of control.

"Look!" Jen said, happily staring out the window. "The skiing is going to be so awesome. I can't wait!"

"I can't wait for the babes on the mountain to check out my shredding style on the half-pipe," Pacey said excitedly.

Joey saw Dawson give her a quick glance. "Yeah. I think I'll board, too. It will be a great way to meet girls."

"Ride—not board," Pacey corrected. "But don't worry, I'll teach you all the lingo." Pacey took a hand off the steering wheel and gave Dawson a high-five. "It's going to be a babe-fest. I can feel it in my bones."

"Do they have that many mountain goats in Vermont?" Joey cracked, finding the opportunity to rag on Pacey hard to resist. But she stopped herself from going on. She didn't want Dawson to think his comment about meeting new girls had made her jealous. She wasn't. She actually wanted someone to come along and take his mind off of her for a while.

They drove on, and Pacey tuned in to a college radio station playing cool tunes. As Joey bopped her head along to the beat, her eyes drank in the flat farms they passed, sheeted in white snow so pure it looked like carpeting. She thought the towering bare trees, looming with their branches out-stretched, looked like tall, elegant tango dancers.

As they worked their way up the winding mountain road, Joey peered out the window at the view of quaint barns and snowy cliffs below. The pictur-esque scene warmed her heart. She had never been to Vermont before, but this was exactly how she pictured it.

Slowly, charming wooden houses of a small vil-lage came into view. They passed a stately white church with a huge pointed steeple that was like so many New England chapels Joey had seen. Further along, several inns dotted the narrow route, with cozy sounding names like the Humble Hearth, the Snowflake Lodge, Innsbruck Inn, and Green Moun-tain Guest House. Signs boasting antiques, crafts, homemade pies, and maple syrup intermingled with others announcing "No Vacancy."

Twists of smoke poured out of chimneys of some old-fashioned private homes. Joey pictured people sitting around a fireplace, sharing easy conversation and hot chocolate.

"We're almost there!" Jen enthused. "Only about ten more minutes."

Jen pointed out Steep Mountain, which rose out of the horizon, standing guard over the small town at its base. It looked enormous, and it certainly was aptly named, Joey thought. She could see the white paths trailing down the side. She wondered if she'd ever be able to ski down one of those.

Jen went on to direct Pacey to the cabin. Joey had to admit, he was doing a great job driving. She didn't have to panic once, even on the steep, winding roads. But of course, she wouldn't let him know that.

Soon, Pacey turned into a narrow dirt road and flicked on the headlights. It was getting dark now, and Joey was glad they were almost there.

"Go all the way to the end of the road. It sits right at the foot of the cul-de-sac," Jen instructed.

Before they knew it, the headlights illuminated the most adorable little house Joey had ever seen. It was a decent-sized cabin, shingled all in wood with hunter green shutters and a peaked roof. A large screened-in porch, furnished with all sorts of rockers and wooden chairs, welcomed them in the front.

"We're here!" Jen cried. "Welcome to the Lindley Chalet!"

"Wahoo!" Pacey whooped as he pulled up the drive. He turned the ignition off, and the gang popped open their doors and scrambled out of the car.

"Excellent driving, my man," Dawson said, patting Pacey on the back. "You got us here safely and in good time. My dad would be proud."

"I agree," Jen said. "Good job."

Pacey lifted his eyebrows and looked at Joey for a reaction. She looked down at the ground. "Yeah," she uttered, not believing she was about to compliment the boy who loved to needle her most. "Good driving."

"It's been a pleasure serving you," Pacey said proudly. He reached into the car to pop the trunk. Joey and Jen tromped back and picked out their bags.

Just when she hoisted her backpack from the trunk, Joey felt something cold and wet hit her hair. Then again, and again.

Joey shrieked. Out of nowhere, she and Jen were getting clobbered with fluffy snowballs.

The girls dropped their bags and exchanged decisive looks. "This is war!" Jen declared.

Joey scooped up some snow and instantly packed it tight into a ball.

Wham! She got Dawson right in the face. She and Jen laughed at his stunned expression.

"Dead on target," Joey said gleefully.

"Great shot!" Jen agreed.

They scrambled to make more snowballs as they crept to the other side of the car. The Leery family sedan was the perfect shield from the boys' attack.

Joey popped her head up to toss a snowball over. *Thwack!* She too was hit smack in the face.

Giggling, Jen dipped her hands into the snow and splashed it up, showering a pile onto the boys. Joey continued to bomb them with hard-packed balls, until Dawson and Pacey cowered in retreat.

But Dawson dove down suddenly, catching Joey—and her leg—by surprise. He tugged her down in the snow. She fell down into it, feeling like she was falling into a cloud.

"Truce! Let's make angels!" Jen called out, as she

flopped backward into a drift. Everyone followed suit, frantically waving their arms and legs in the snow.

Joey's heart filled with joy. She and Bessie had loved making snow angels when they were little. She stood to examine them and laughed. "They look like four paper dolls," she said, as rose-tinted childhood memories flooded through her. It was scary, she realized, how she already forgot what it was like to be a child. She would give anything to have those good days back again.

Jen brushed snow off her jeans. "Let's go inside and change these wet clothes," she suggested. "But I want to give a quick tour first."

She lifted her bag and walked over to the garage, where she punched in a code on a keypad to open the automatic door. Once inside, she took a set of keys off a hook, unlocked a door that led inside the house, then motioned for everyone to follow her.

First, she led them into a small hallway, with wooden pegs and cubbies. "This is where to put your skis and boots and stuff," Jen explained.

They then stepped into a kitchen/dining area, decorated with homey wooden furniture. Mauve stenciled hearts and flowers bordered the tops and bottoms of the walls, and shiny copper pots and pans hung over the stove. "Is your mother Martha Stewart?" Joey asked, regarding all the cookware.

Jen laughed. "Certainly not! It's all for show. My mom doesn't cook at all. Hates it." She turned a spotless pot toward Joey, to show her the bottom. "Look how clean and shiny these are. Never used." Then she walked to the refrigerator and pulled it open. "Just as I thought," she said. "Empty. We'll have to do some food shopping. But there's spaghetti and jarred sauce in the cupboard for tonight."

She led them to the family room, which was wood-paneled and decorated with accents of burgundy and hunter green. Right in the middle of the far wall was a fireplace. "After we change we can build a fire to warm up," Jen said.

"This is a great place, Jen," Dawson remarked. "It was such a great idea to come here."

"And it's so nice of your parents to let us stay," Joey added, while Pacey nodded in agreement.

"They're turning into softies in their old age," Jen joked as she led them past a staircase and to a closed door. She paused dramatically with her hand on the doorknob. "And this is the best room of all," she said. With a flourish, she threw open the door. There, sitting in the middle of the room, was a nice, big, hot tub.

"Oh my god!" Pacey breathed. "Bring on the babes! I'm ready to jump in right now."

"Uh . . ." Dawson said, a twinge of embarrassment in his voice. "I didn't exactly bring a bathing suit . . ."

"Me neither," Joey said, crestfallen.

"No problem!" Pacey said, rubbing his hands together. "Skinny dipping in the tub! Count me in!"

"If you plan on going in there unclothed, just alert me so I can stay as far away from this room as possible," Joey said.

Jen laughed. "While that sounds fun, we don't have to worry. My parents usually leave suits here. My dad's suits will be a little big for you guys, but they'll do the job. And I think I have a few old ones around."

"Rats," Pacey said dejectedly.

"We can still enjoy it. But I have to turn it on first," Jen said, going over to the tub and flicking a switch. The sound of bubbling filled the room. "We need to give it a while to warm up."

Then she headed for the stairs to show everyone their bedrooms. "There are four, so we each get our own room," Jen pointed out.

Joey followed Jen up the stairs, looking around the place in wonder. She dropped her bag in her room and peeled off her wet clothing.

A cozy cabin, a toasty fireplace, a relaxing hot tub, and her own room, all right off the ski mountain. Not to mention, no Ice House or crying nephews in the middle of the night. Vermont was already everything she had hoped. Now, she was truly ready for a wonderful weekend.

Chapter 4

Jen unpacked her bag and pulled on long johns and a thermal shirt. Now that she was dry and comfortable, her stomach rumbled with hunger. She thought it would be a good idea to whip up that spaghetti.

She trotted down the stairs and into the kitchen. Opening up a cupboard, she found the sauce and pasta where it was always stored. She pulled them out, set a pot of water on the stove, then opened the sauce and dumped it into another pot.

"Mmmm," Pacey said, coming up behind her. "I'm hungry from all of that excellent driving," he said. "I hope all of you unlicensed drivers took note of how it's done, from the supreme driving skills I displayed."

"Listen, Rain Man," Joey said, as she stepped into the kitchen. "Don't get cocky. It's not nuclear physics."

"After we go food shopping we can really whip up some fun meals," Jen said, deflecting a Pacey-Joey showdown. As Dawson trailed in, she added, "This will be ready in a few minutes."

Pacey, Dawson, and Joey set the table as Jen fussed with the last minutes of the pasta preparation. She dished it out into painted pottery bowls, and the gang sat around the wooden dining table, chattering about plans for the weekend.

"There are some cool hangouts in town," Jen said. "And in the base lodge at the mountain, there's an excellent little pub with a big, roaring fire and live entertainment at the end of every day." She regarded Joey. "Lots of cute ski-bum types are known to hang there après-ski. Makes for excellent scoping."

Joey smiled wide. "Great!" she answered enthusiastically.

Jen noticed Dawson's grim expression. He was a hopeless case, she thought. It seemed that Joey wasn't the least bit interested in him. Sooner or later he would get tired of pining after her—she hoped.

"So, is there a TV?" Pacey asked as he dug into the pasta. *The Simpsons* is on tonight."

Jen shook her head. "Unfortunately, my parents wanted this to be a real getaway. They were upset when they had to break down and get a phone, so they could be reached in an emergency when my grandfather was sick. But," she added, "we can play some old-fashioned board games."

"Sounds great," Dawson said.

They all gobbled the spaghetti with gusto, finishing it in record time, Jen noted. She was having a great time with her good friends, and was so happy to share a place that meant a lot to her with them.

Dawson, Joey, and Pacey insisted on cleaning up, so Jen strolled into the family room to find a good game to play. She opened up a cupboard in the wall unit near the fireplace, and checked out the games. She read their titles out loud, as an interested Pacey walked over and peered over her shoulder.

"We have Scrabble," she started.

"Ick," Pacey responded. "I don't want to play anything that requires too much thinking."

She went on, listing the names of the games. "Monopoly. Clue. Balderdash. Scattergories, and . . ." She paused, saying the last title uncertainly. "Foreplay?"

"I want to play that one," Pacey said, grabbing the box from the cupboard. "Learn your friends' most intimate sexual secrets," he read in his best announcer voice. "Cool!"

"I don't know where that one came from," Jen said. "It was never here before. And there are some other weird games, too: Hush-hush. Touch and Tickle. Where did these come from?"

Pacey wiggled his eyebrows. "I guess your parents have a good old time when they come here."

Dawson laughed. "Let me see that," he said, walking over and reaching for the box marked "Foreplay."

"How about Balderdash?" Joey asked as she stepped into the family room. "I like that game."

Dawson laughed again, reading the box. "No way. We're playing this one. 'Answer intimate questions. Divulge your secret fantasies. Take off an article of clothing.' " He gave Pacey a high-five. "This is definitely going to make for some fine entertainment."

Jen sighed, uncomfortable with the whole idea. Playing this game was exactly the type of shenanigans her grandmother was expecting of them. She remembered the lecture she had gotten before she left the house for school in the morning. "Don't break anything. Don't bring strangers into the house. And no parties," Grams had said.

Jen shot Joey a look. She figured there was no way that Joey would play this game. She was so modest.

"I'll set up the board," Pacey said. "Why don't we light a fire—get in the mood," he said seductively.

"Well, I hope you and Dawson have fun," Jen said. "Because we're not going to play. Right, Joey?"

Jen watched as Joey looked from the boys' eager faces to Jen's own disapproving glare. "Right?" she repeated meekly.

Joey shook her head. "No," she said cheerily. "Let's play. I think this sounds like fun."

Jen shrugged. She didn't want to seem like a prude, which was probably why Joey wanted to play. *Whatever*, she thought. She just wanted all of her guests to be comfortable. She wasn't inhibited in the least. She shouldn't have any problem at all with this game.

Dawson took out the instructions and read them aloud. "Okay. Set up the board. Roll the dice to move forward. There are five types of spaces to land on: Question, Task, Toss-up, Free Pass, or Lose a Turn. When you land on a Question space, you must answer the question. When you land on the

Task space, you must do what the card says. When you land on Toss-up, you can choose which card to answer." Dawson raised his eyebrows as he continued. "When you land on Lose a Turn, you not only lose a turn but you lose an article of clothing. Hot stuff!"

"Whoo!" Jen said, trying to get into the spirit of the game. "What about Free Pass? What does that mean?"

Dawson continued reading. "The lucky person who lands on the Free Pass gets to keep a card and weasel out of a question, task, or lost turn by passing it to someone else. The first player to reach the end of the board wins. Note: it is important to tell the truth. Another player can challenge your credibility. In that case, the other players vote on whether they think you are telling the truth, and then the accused rolls to see how many items of clothing he or she has to remove. Wow," he added incredulously. "This is going to be fun."

"No kidding," Pacey said. "I hope you girls aren't wearing a lot of layers. Be prepared . . ."

"I guess we'll need a microscope," Joey responded, "if you end up taking it all off."

"Not necessary," he said defensively.

"We'll see about that," Jen added coyly.

"Let's get started," Dawson insisted, eager to play.

They set up the board on the coffee table in the family room, right next to the fire, which was already throwing a raging heat.

Jen admired the way shadows from the flames flickered on Dawson's handsome face. And the more she thought about it, the more she realized that this game might make for some good flirting opportunities.

"Okay, who goes first," Pacey said, also anxious to get the show on the road. He picked up the die and rolled. "Six! Beat that," he said to Joey, passing the die over to her.

"Four," Joey said after her roll. Jen was next, and she rolled a one. Dawson went last and got a five. Pacey would start the game.

"Here we go!" Pacey said. "Baby needs a new pair of shoes!" he shouted as he shook the die in his hands and tossed it. It bounced off the board and into the woodpile. "Do over," he said, scrambling to find it.

"We're not playing craps," Joey complained. "All you have to do is drop it on the board."

"Okay, okay," Pacey said, pulling the cube out of the woodpile. He rolled again. Three. He took his piece and plunked it on the squares. When he put his piece on the correct spot, his face fell. He didn't like what he saw.

Jen and Joey burst into laughter and gave each other a high-five.

"Lose a turn!" Jen shouted. "Lose a piece of clothing!"

"Couldn't happen to a nicer guy," Joey said. "Just don't reveal too much. I just ate."

Jen noticed that Pacey seemed embarrassed. But he sucked in his breath and steeled himself. "No big deal," he said, searching his body for what to remove. He wore gray sweatpants, a white T-shirt, and not much else. "The shirt," he said, pulling it over his head.

"Good thing we have a fire going, pal," Dawson joked. "You'd be frozen stiff already."

Jen admired Pacey's physique. Not bad, she thought. Not bad at all. Though he wasn't especially "built," he had a nicely defined chest and biceps for his slender but athletic frame.

"You're next, Ms. Potter," Pacey said, offering Joey the die.

Joey rolled, praying to get anything but a three. "Four," she said, relieved, then moved her piece to a square marked Free Pass. "Yes!" Joey cheered triumphantly, raising a fist into the air. She eagerly took the card and kept it.

Jen was up next. She hoped she'd be as lucky as Joey. She shook the die and rolled a two. Carefully, she moved her piece on the space marked Question. She was relieved; at least she didn't have to shed any clothing. She just hoped the question wouldn't be too embarrassing.

Pacey pulled a question card out of the box. "Allow me," he said. He cleared his throat and read: "What is the craziest, sexiest thing you've ever done in public?" he asked.

Jen was quiet for a few seconds. Her wild days in New York gave her many answers to that one.

All eyes were on Jen as she searched her memory for something fun, but not too risqué.

"You have to answer," Pacey prompted. "And tell the truth—or else it can get mighty cold in here."

"Okay, okay," Jen said, thinking quickly. "In Manhattan there's a bar called Bulls and Steers. It's a down-and-dirty biker joint. It was quite fashionable—a lot of celebrities used to hang out there, even though it was a dive in the smelly meatpacking district—"

Pacey mock yawned. "Ho hum."

"I'm getting to the good part," Jen assured him. "It's not unusual there for women to remove their tops and jump on the bar to dance—"

"What was the name of this place?" Dawson asked, suddenly perking up with interest.

"Bulls and Steers," Jen answered.

"What street is it on?" Pacey asked.

Jen waved his question away impatiently. "That's not important. Let me finish the story. So, one night, on a dare, I joined in on the fun. I took off my shirt, jumped on the bar, and danced in my bra for everyone to see."

Dawson and Pacey stared at Jen, open-mouthed, while Joey regarded her with a combination of shock and respect. "Wow," Joey said. "That's pretty brave. Didn't any of the guys hassle you?"

Jen shook her head. "I was there with my boyfriend. And Bruno, the bouncer, always kept a good eye on me."

"I bet he did!" Pacey chimed in, then he burst into applause. "That was a good one. Dawson, you're next."

"All right," Dawson said, giving the die a good shake and toss. He also rolled a two, which put him on the Question space.

This time, Jen pulled a Question card out. "Describe your fantasy mate," she read.

Dawson paused and smiled. "Good one," he said, then deliberated thoughtfully. "Well, she's smart, for one thing. And beautiful," he went on, then paused again. "I like a girl who pulls no punches—one who gives it to you straight. And I like someone who's loyal."

Jen saw Dawson catch Joey's eye, then continue, locking her in his look. "I think my fantasy woman is someone with whom I feel comfortable. Someone in whom I can confide. Someone who knows all of my secrets. Most importantly, she's someone I can call my best friend."

Wake up and smell the latte, Jen thought. He was obviously describing Joey. Jen could tell by the way Joey blushed and looked away that Dawson's answer made her really uncomfortable.

But Pacey came to the rescue. "Good enough. My turn again," he said, breaking the tension. He tossed the die and moved four more spaces. "Question," he said. He wiped a hand across his forehead in an exaggerated expression of relief.

Joey reached to pull a card out of the box. "Name the most unusual place you've ever made out," she read.

"Easy," Pacey quickly answered. "That would be in the classroom."

Jen knew that was all too true; he must have seen some action in school with Miss Jacobs. "We won't challenge you there," she said.

Joey rolled next. "Two," she said, then counted out the spaces. "Task."

Dawson took a task card and read it. He smiled confidently. "Tell a member of the opposite sex what his or her best physical attribute is."

Jen stifled laughter at the sinking look on Joey's face. She was in some pickle! Jen knew that she

probably didn't want to lead Dawson on by compli-
menting him, but at the same time, it might kill her
to say something nice to Pacey.

But Jen didn't have a lot of sympathy for Joey;
she wanted to play this game, after all. She figured
Joey would get out of the situation by turning in her
Free Pass.

But Jen was surprised when Joey turned to Pacey
and spoke.

"You have an above-average butt," Joey mumbled.

"What?" Pacey said, a sly grin creeping across his
face. "I didn't hear what you said?"

"I'm not repeating it," Joey snapped.

Jen laughed out loud.

"What's so funny?" Pacey asked.

Jen stopped laughing. "Nothing," she said. "The
whole thing just caught me off-guard." That was
true, but even funnier was Pacey's smug smile,
Joey's embarrassed grimace, and Dawson's bewildered scowl.

"Credibility challenge!" Dawson suddenly shouted.
"I don't think you're telling the truth."

Jen stepped to Joey's defense. It wasn't a lie, after
all, and Dawson shouldn't challenge an answer just
because he wasn't happy with it. "That's not necessary, Dawson. I'll vouch for her. It is the truth."

Dawson bit his lip. "This game does not foster
mature responses," he said bitterly.

"The girls can't help it," Pacey bellowed, standing
up, turning around, and wiggling his rear end. "The
babes dig my booty."

"Enough," Joey said, rolling her eyes. "I said
above-average. Don't get carried away."

"With any luck you gals will be able to see it up close and personal—"

"With any luck someone will come in and stick a ski boot in your mouth," Joey retorted. "Size twelve."

"My turn," Jen cut in, averting any further arguments. She rolled the die, and landed on a Task square.

Pacey sat down and whipped out a card. "Go up to a member of the opposite sex and kiss him or her on the mouth," he read. He put the card down. "I'll even throw in a butt-squeeze for free, if you'd like."

But Jen wasn't planning on kissing Pacey, that was for sure. This was her opportunity to steal a kiss from Dawson—something she'd be longing to do for some time.

She moved over next to Dawson, who glared at Joey smugly. Without another word, Jen placed her mouth on Dawson's soft lips. Slowly, they kissed.

Jen felt a familiar warm feeling all throughout her body and her heart felt so full it might burst.

"A-hem," Pacey said, after a full minute. "I think you've completed the task satisfactorily."

Jen slowly pulled away from Dawson, whose brown eyes sparkled with tenderness. Jen's whole body tingled, and her heart hammered in her chest. There was no doubt; it was a great kiss.

If she wasn't sure before, now she was. She wanted more of those kisses. She wanted Dawson back. Content, Jen breathed a happy sigh, then crawled back to her spot at the end of the coffee table.

She noticed Joey's irritated sidelong glance at her. Was that a spark of jealousy she saw in her eyes?

Dawson rolled, still flushed from the kiss. "Question," he said.

Joey pulled a card out, and stifled a giggle before she read it. She cleared her throat. "True or false. You are the jealous type."

"False," Dawson said confidently. "Definitely false."

Jen and Joey shot each other looks and burst out laughing.

"What?" Dawson said. "It's true! I am not jealous!"

"Definite credibility challenge," Joey said between laughs, slapping the card down.

"I second that," Jen added. Dawson had looked like he would nearly detonate when Joey told Pacey that he had a nice butt. And Jen had more than one run-in with his jealousy when they were dating. There was the time when her ex-boyfriend Billy came to visit—and Dawson became a wreck. And he had caused a scene when she went to the school dance with Cliff Elliot. There were too many times to count.

"No!" Dawson said. "You guys are lying." He turned to Pacey. "Help me out, man. Tell them that they're wrong."

Pacey slowly shook his head. "I hate to do it to you, my friend," he said. "But I have to tell the truth. The girls are right. I'm afraid you are a teeny-weeny bit on the possessive side."

"Fine! This game is so stupid!" Dawson said, his brown eyes flickering with annoyance.

"Who wanted to play it?" Joey challenged.

Jen tried to calm Dawson. "It's just a game," she reminded him. "And you have to roll to see how many articles of clothing you lose," she added.

Dawson grumbled and picked up the die. "Four!" he shouted. "I'm going to freeze to death!" he protested.

"It's not that bad," a shirtless Pacey assured him.

Dawson pulled off one sock, then another. "These count as two," he said, flicking one each at Jen and Joey.

"Okay," Joey said, tossing the sock aside. "No one is saying otherwise."

Then he pulled off his sweatshirt. Underneath, he wore a T-shirt, which he also took off.

Dawson slumped backward, shirtless, sockless, but still wearing jeans. "Next," he said impatiently.

It was Pacey's turn. He rolled excitedly, then slapped his forehead when he advanced his piece. Three: lose a turn.

"Ha, ha!" Jen laughed gleefully.

"Okay, ladies. This one's for you," Pacey said as he peeled off his sweatpants, with a bump and a grind. "It's too bad for you that I'm wearing underwear. Maybe next roll you'll get lucky."

"We'll live in nauseous, horrified anticipation until then," Joey said. "Now it's my turn."

She rolled. "Five," she said, moving her piece. "Question."

Pacey picked out the card this time. "Okay, Madame." He silently read it. "Oh, this is so boring! You guys get all the easy questions!"

"Just read it," Joey insisted.

Pacey sighed. "Are you currently in love?"

Jen watched Joey's face fall, her expression suddenly uncomfortable. At the same time, a confident smirk disappeared as quickly as it appeared on Dawson's face.

"I repeat," Pacey said. "Are you currently in lo—"

"I heard the question the first time," Joey snapped. She picked up her Free Pass and handed it to Jen. "Here. I pass."

Dawson's eyes widened. "What?" he asked, his voice wavering. He sounded annoyed. "You won't answer that? That's ridiculous! It's an easy question!"

"I don't have to answer it. I had a Free Pass," Joey said defensively. "The only person who has to answer it is Jen."

Dawson shot Joey a hurt look. "I can't believe you're refusing to discuss this with us. I mean, we're your best friends," he said. He stood, pulling his sweatshirt back on. "This game is for totally immature people who have no capability for intelligent conversation themselves," he muttered as he stalked out of the room.

Joey put her head in her hand, feeling Jen and Pacey's shocked stares on her. She collected her thoughts, then stood up after a minute to go after him.

Pacey gave Jen a sheepish look when Joey skulked out of the room. "Guess this wasn't a great idea after all," he said.

"No," Jen answered. "Not at all."

Dawson slammed the door to his room, then sat on the bed. He turned around and punched the puffy crimson-red pillow—it was the same color as the bright turtleneck that Joey wore that evening. He just didn't understand what was with her. Was she going out of her way to make him angry tonight? And why couldn't she answer that simple little question? Was she just toying with him or was it possible that she had not been in love with him?

Sure, they were broken up now, Dawson realized, but the pain went on. He wanted to stay close to Joey but he didn't know how much he could take. What was better—a lonely life without Joey or an emotionally tortured life with her? He just didn't know.

He stretched out on the bed and stared at the ceiling, taking a few deep breaths. He had to calm down. It seemed like his plans for winning Joey back were already shot. But he didn't want that to ruin his whole weekend. He still wanted to have fun and he didn't want to agonize over Joey the whole time.

If only he could forget all about her. Meeting new people with Pacey would be a step in the right direction, he figured, but he knew deep in his heart that it would take more than that to erase his feelings for Joey.

Something told him that he would never be able to forget about Joey Potter. How could he? She'd been a part of his life for as long as he could remember.

Dawson sat up when he heard a light tap at the door. He didn't say anything, but he had a pretty good idea of who it was. When the door slowly opened, he could see it was Joey.

"I'm sorry," she said softly, her shiny brown hair hanging down over her shoulders, looking so lustrous that Dawson wanted to stroke it. "It was a stupid game. I guess we're not as recovered from our . . . thing . . . as we thought."

"Our *thing*?" Dawson asked miserably, sitting up. "Is that what you call it?" He asked, feeling his anger rise again.

Joey walked into the room and sat next to Dawson. "I meant our relationship," she explained. "I just want us to get past those feelings. We'd been over this so many times. It's not right for us right now . . . I think you know that. We're too close. I think we have to stop flip-flopping like this. And I don't want to go to extremes . . ."

Dawson shook his head. "I don't want to let you go," he said sadly. "And I don't want to drive you away, either. It's just so hard. I have so many feelings for you. I was hoping that we'd—" he stopped, searching for the right word, "—reconnect after this weekend."

"We can't, Dawson," Joey said. "I'm sorry." At Dawson's crestfallen expression, she added, "Look, I have feelings for you, too. It's just that I'm not exactly sure what they are—or mean. I need more experience to figure out what we have. And I want to be fair to you, so I don't think it's right that we should get back together." She stopped, letting out a breath. "For now."

"So, am I supposed to sit around like a dolt and wait for you to come around?" Dawson asked desperately.

"No," Joey said, standing up to leave. "Please don't do that. I don't expect you to."

"Wait, Joey—" Dawson said urgently, as she pulled open the door. "There's something I have to know."

Joey paused, crossing her arms over her chest, a look of trepidation on her pretty face. "What is it?"

Dawson knew he shouldn't ask this question, but he just had to know. "I know you said that you always loved me," he said.

Joey's shoulders fell, and her expression grew helpless.

"Well," Dawson pressed. "I need to know. Did you really mean it? Did our time together mean anything to you?"

"Of course it meant something to me, but things are different now."

When Joey passed the master bedroom, Jen made herself look busy, unpacking and hanging clothes in the closet. She felt sorry for Dawson, and she wanted to console him; he seemed so wounded and fragile. But at the same time, she wanted to slap some sense into him, too. He was so hung up on Joey—just the way he'd been hung up on her the year before. Why did he have to throw himself so fiercely into every relationship? His romantic-tortured-sensitive-artist bit was wearing thin. He didn't have to be hurt so much of the time.

Then again, it was easy for Jen, who wouldn't get involved enough to allow herself to be hurt, to feel that way. Maybe that's why her romantic life had been one big dud lately. But did she really want to be intensely involved with Dawson? Or did she just miss having an attentive boyfriend? She didn't know.

Jen turned her attention back to hanging things in the closet. Now that she was concentrating on this task, and not listening in on Dawson and Joey's conversation, she could see that there were clothes already in there. Pulling a hanger toward her, Jen examined the closet's contents.

The closet contained women's clothes. But strangely, they weren't Jen's mother's clothes—or at least they didn't appear to be. They were all about two sizes smaller than what her mom usually wore; and it hadn't been *that* long since Jen had seen her—certainly not long enough to go down two dress sizes.

And it wasn't only the sizes that disturbed her: it was the types of clothes. A slinky, ultrashort black dress; several sexy satin and lace robes; longer dresses with thigh-revealing slits; low-cut silky-sheer blouses. Jen mused that these were the exact opposite taste to her Mom's sensible, conservative style.

But if they weren't her mother's, whose clothes were they?

Jen tried not to dwell on it as she crawled into bed and flicked out the light. She was just too tired, and she was looking forward to resting up and getting an excellent night's sleep. And she really didn't want to know.

Pacey flipped through his *Sports Illustrated*, too excited to get to sleep. He couldn't wait for tomorrow. He closed his eyes and anticipated what the day might hold for him: layers of untrodden white, fluffy snow, just waiting for him to shred it up. A gaggle of girls fighting to ride to the top of the mountain with him. A cool, mountain breeze brushing his face as he raced down the slope.

He put down his magazine and laid his head on the pillow. The best part of the trip was being away from home. No overcrowded house, full of chaos. No Doug. No Dad. No rules. No Screenplay Video. And no school.

He could certainly get used to being away from it all. He fantasized about not going back; staying on Steep Mountain, giving snowboard lessons to pretty young girls. That would be his dream life, he

thought. If only he had the money—and the guts—
to do it.

He was determined to get Dawson to loosen up,
especially after what had happened earlier in the
evening with Joey. It would be good for Dawson to
get some attention from new girls, not to mention
that it would be easier to meet girls in general as a
duo. Plus, if Dawson met someone new, Pacey
wouldn't have to listen to him moan about Joey the
whole weekend.

Meeting new and exciting people. Riding his
board. Being on his own. Pacey reached up and
turned out the light and shut his eyes, eager to
dream about the white, winter mountains.

In the magical alpines of Vermont, he couldn't
wait to see what tomorrow would bring.

Joey laced up her boots and quietly slipped outside. The cool night air sent shivers up her spine as
she zipped up her ski jacket. Maybe coming here
wasn't such a great idea after all, she thought. She
should have known that this kind of proximity to
Dawson would cause freak-outs of major proportions.

But it wasn't just Dawson. Joey realized that she
deserved part of the blame for their inexplicable romantic dynamics. For example, she had to admit
that she didn't like it one bit when Dawson and Jen
were kissing during the game. It brought back the
all-too-familiar feelings of envy she had when Jen
was dating Dawson.

She wished they had never played Foreplay. She
thought it would be fun at first—a good excuse for
her to let her hair down. But, they all should have

learned their lessons from that time they played Truth-or-Dare in the library during detention. Games that took any more thought than checkers were not good to play in mixed company.

Joey circled the house, her boots crunching on the hardening snow. The temperature was dropping rapidly, and the night was growing darker. But she just couldn't seem to get to sleep. She figured that a walk, and a little time to herself, would clear her mind.

Dawson Leery was a piece of work. Her heart told her to run to him, clutch him, and never let him go. But her head told her that she was too young to get so wrapped up in a guy—especially one she had known all her life. How could she limit herself like that?

She turned onto the driveway and, kicking an ice ball, walked out to the dirt road. Joey thought about how her father had let her mother down so many times. Even before her mother was sick, he failed her, he cheated on her, and deserted them all before he finally ended up in jail.

Joey had to admit her dad action's put a dent in her ability to trust people, especially men. How did she know that it wouldn't happen to her? If things got serious with Dawson, would he let her down, too?

But a little, tiny voice that Joey could barely hear told her that all men weren't like her father. The voice also whispered that she should give Dawson another chance.

Joey blew out puffs of smoky winter night air. No, she told herself. She had already made up her mind.

She didn't want anything serious. She wanted fun. That way she was sure not to be let down.

She turned around on the dirt road, realizing that she had been so lost in her thoughts that the cabin was no longer in view. She didn't want to get lost.

Joey figured that she should find her way back and get to sleep. They were going to get an early start the next day, and she didn't want to be grouchy from lack of sleep. She stuck her bare hands into her pockets, and trudged up the road back toward "Lindley Chalet."

Tomorrow, she would spend the morning taking lessons, away from Dawson and all the emotional confusion. Maybe she'd spend some time alone later on in the afternoon. It comforted her to have that to look forward to.

One thing was for sure: Joey decided that she wasn't going to let Dawson, or her feelings for him, ruin her weekend. She was determined to have fun, no matter what it took.

Chapter 6

"Fresh Powder!" Pacey cheered as he ran out to the car the following morning. The snow drifted gracefully onto the ground, dusting the air around him. Pacey opened his arms out wide. "I can't wait! We're going to catch some big air today," he said to Dawson. "I can feel it."

Jen emerged from the cabin carrying her skis and boots. She wore a fashionable, sleek black jumpsuit, trimmed with shocking pink and magenta stripes. Pacey noticed how it showed off all of her curves. He hoped he would be seeing a lot of similar curves—on and off the trails today.

Joey trailed behind Jen, closing the door of the cabin as she left. She wore jeans and her royal blue winter parka and was much less of a snow bunny in her simple, earthy style. "Are we going to be able to fit all of our rental stuff in the car?" she asked no one in particular.

"I don't think it should be a problem," Dawson said. "We had Jen's skis and Pacey's board on the way up, and I'm only renting a board. There should be plenty of room for your stuff."

"Terje is already snugly in there," Pacey said, opening the trunk and placing Jen's skis inside. He was relieved to see that Dawson and Joey were acting normal this morning. They seemed to be making a big effort today to be comfortable around each other.

"Terje?" Joey asked.

"Terje Haakenson—champion snowboarder from Norway. The best the world's ever seen," Pacey explained.

"He's in the trunk?" Jen joked, peeking over Pacey's shoulder.

Pacey laughed. "No! I named my board after him!"

"How . . . weird," Joey remarked.

Pacey shrugged her comment off. Nothing could put him in a bad mood today—not even Joey's quips. He couldn't wait to hit the slopes. Steep Mountain was a great mountain for riding. It even had a half-pipe for tricks and stunts.

Pacey had purchased his board last year, along with his brand-new black baggy pants that hung loosely from his frame, allowing for optimum movement. He also bought a brand-new electric-green jacket and comfortable soft boots. He couldn't wait to put all the new equipment to use.

They piled into the car and Pacey slowly drove down the dirt road. The snow started tapering off. Good, he thought. Better visibility.

He carefully wound the car around to the path that led them to the base lodge. Normally, they wouldn't have to drive. They could take a trail from Jen's yard directly to the mountain. But since Joey and Dawson needed to rent, they had to drive down to the base lodge.

The parking lot was filling up, even though it was only eight o'clock in the morning. "Looks like there's going to be a crowd today," Dawson pointed out.

"Always is on holiday weekends," Jen answered.

Once they parked, Pacey popped the trunk and carefully lifted his board out, running his fingers along the smooth, hard edges. "Okay, Terje baby. Let's get ready to meet some Shred Bettys."

Joey scoffed. "What in the world does that mean?" she asked as she came up next to him.

"Shred Bettys are girl riders," Pacey answered.

"Oh. Whatever. Snowboarding sounds so mature," Joey responded.

They walked up to a large gray, barnlike building that sported a huge iron weathervane on top. Pacey approached a small line by a window and stopped. "Is this where we buy lift tickets?" he asked.

Jen nodded. She indicated a door to the right of it. "Then we go in there. This is the base lodge. Upstairs are the pub, cafeteria, and lounge. Downstairs are the rental shop and the apparel shop. Keep me away from the apparel shop. Every time I go in there I buy more ski stuff I don't need."

"Don't worry. I won't be able to afford anything, so I plan on staying away myself," Joey said.

After they bought their lift tickets, Jen led the way

into the rental shop. Pacey admired the brand-new boards they had available for rent and was impressed by their quality. But none of them were as good as Terje, he concluded.

"I am definitely boarding," Dawson said.

"*Riding*, Dawson," Pacey reminded him. "Only neophyte dweebs say 'boarding.' Got it?"

"Sorry, man," Dawson said. "I've only done it a few times. I can hold my own on the slopes but I don't have the lingo down yet."

"That's all right," Pacey said, patting him on the back. "Just stick with me and I'll teach you all the right things to say."

As Jen helped Joey pick out skis, boots, and poles, Pacey counseled Dawson on choosing a good board. "You want a freeride board," Pacey told him. "It's a great all-in-one board."

"Okay," Dawson said. "And I prefer soft boots as opposed to hard."

The attendant nodded, taking Dawson's form and walking away to retrieve his equipment.

"Your jacket should be perfect for riding," Pacey mentioned, admiring Dawson's army-green shell.

"I hate the jackets that make you look like a puffed out snowman. This was loose and comfortable," Dawson responded, "and warmer than it looks."

The attendant returned with Dawson's gear. After checking it all out, the boys were ready to roll. They strolled over to the counter where Jen and Joey were still waiting.

"We're going to be a little while yet," Jen told the boys. "Why don't you guys go on ahead. I'll get Joey set up with her lessons and maybe I'll catch you on the slopes later."

"Sounds good," Pacey said, giving her the thumbs up. "Have fun."

"If I don't see you on the slopes then let's meet in the pub after the lifts close—by the big fireplace if it's too crowded—around four o'clockish. We'll hang and listen to the live music," Jen added.

"Cool," Dawson said. He turned to Pacey. "Let's do it, man. Let's boar—I mean ride! I want to shred up the mountain."

Pacey smiled. Now Dawson was showing the spirit he had hoped for. "Watch out Steep Mountain," he said. "Here we come!"

Chapter 7

"**W**ait! You're walking too fast!" Joey struggled through the snow in her ski boots, awkwardly balancing her skis and poles in her hands. She looked helplessly over at Jen, who strode confidently, with every hair in place, not the least bit frazzled by lugging her skis around. She stopped and waited for Joey to catch up.

"Thanks," Joey said, practically tripping over her skis. As she plodded on, she noticed a yellow-and-black sign that said Ski School. Finally, they were there. She was exhausted before she even had her first lesson.

Joey regarded the hill. It was more like a snowdrift. But she was happy about that—it was just her speed. What she wasn't so happy about were the swarms of kids crowding around. Her heart sank when she realized she was the only one over eight years old. "Why did I sign up for group lessons?" she asked.

Jen grimaced. "Private lessons are more expensive. But they might have been worth it for you."

Joey let out a breath, picturing herself tripping over the screaming little brats. "Great. This is going to be so embarrassing. No doubt these kids are going to be better than me."

"Well, look on the bright side," Jen said. "The instructor might give you a lollipop if you do well."

"Not funny," Joey said dryly.

Joey dropped her skis and poles as a woman with a clipboard checked them in. "I'm Joey. Joey Potter," she said, as Jen helped her slip into her bindings.

The woman looked surprised. "Oh!" she said, looking down at her clipboard and flipping through a few pages. "Oh, dear. I guess your paper smudged." She held it up for Joey to see. In the age box on her registration form, only the number 5 was visible, the 1 in 15 had a water droplet on it.

"I thought you were much younger, so I put you with this group." The woman gave an embarrassed chuckle. "I'm afraid that the adult group already left. They hopped on a jitney to the other bunny hill down the road." She acknowledged the children around her. "More private, less noisy. No people looking on."

Joey's face fell. So now she would be stuck with the kids' group, a spectacle for all to point at and guffaw. Every time she got her hopes up for a good time, something bizarre happened.

"I'll take her," she heard a deep voice say behind her.

Joey whirled around to see where it came from. She was greeted by a big, white smile, complete with dimples.

"Why don't you take the kids, Joyce. I'll take this young lady," the mysterious young ski instructor said.

Joey returned his smile. He was one of the cutest guys she had ever seen. He had thick, dirty blond hair that hung slightly past his shoulders. A scruffy brown five-o'clock shadow didn't hide his adorable dimples, and a tiny gold hoop hung from his left ear. Joey thought he looked cool and fun—like a surfer or a rock star.

Jen caught Joey's wide eyes and winked.

"I'm Chad," the instructor said, sticking out a gloved hand. "But you can call me Stinky."

Joey and Jen started to laugh.

"Don't get the wrong idea," he said, holding his hands up. "It's because of the way I ride a board. The term for a wide stance is 'stinkbug,' like the bugs whose legs have a stretched-out span. It has nothing to do with my grooming habits."

"We'll be the judge of that," Jen teased. "I'm Jen Lindley. And this is Joey Potter."

"Hey," Joey said, giving him a casual wave.

"Listen," Stinky said, "it was our mistake about the grouping. So, we'll throw in the private lessons for the same price. Okay?"

It was more than okay for Joey. "Great!" she said. She turned to Jen and gave her a proud smile.

"Thanks for helping me out. I think I'm in good hands," she said with a little giggle. "Have fun!"

But Jen didn't seem like she wanted to leave. "Uh—sure," she said, hesitantly. "I guess I'll catch up with you when your lesson is over. I can take you on some of the easy trails after that. When could I swing by?"

"In about three hours," Stinky said. "Right before lunchtime."

"Okay," Jen said, still lingering.

"Go ahead now," Joey said, shooing Jen away. She couldn't wait to get her lesson underway. "You don't want the lift lines to get too crowded. Maybe you can find Dawson and Pacey. Bye!"

Finally, Jen seemed to take the hint. "I'll see you later," she said. "Have fun."

As Joey looked over into Stinky's smiling face, she recalled Jen's last words. Finally, it seemed like fun was something she was going to have.

Pacey and Dawson sat on the chairlift, waiting to get to the top for their first run. As the lift moved higher and higher, Pacey drank in the mountain scenery. Tall, green pines nearly scraped the sky; the majestic snowcapped peaks stood, white and sturdy, around them. The sky was robin's egg blue, unmarred by clouds. The sun shone brightly down on them.

It was the perfect day. It was just cold enough to feel like it was winter, but not unbearably freezing, and there were no skin-chapping Arctic winds. Already, Pacey could tell that the conditions were great. The mountain reported an excellent, deep powder base.

The boys had decided to take a couple of warm-up runs before they hit the half-pipe. The half-pipe was basically for jumps and tricks, which was Pacey's favorite part of riding. He loved to go side to side on the U-shaped tube, building up just the right amount of momentum for a spin, twist, jump, or handstand. Completing any of those moves successfully gave him an outstanding rush.

When the lift reached the top, both Pacey and Dawson expertly dismounted. "Ready, dude?" Pacey asked Dawson.

"Ready," Dawson said, pulling his gloves tight.

Pacey gave his buddy a nod. "You first. We'll take the long blue trail that cuts across. Witch's Broom I think it was called."

"Roger," Dawson answered as he tightened his bindings, then crouched down low so he could glide to the trail entrance.

For someone who skied more than he rode, Dawson was certainly comfortable on a board, Pacey noted. Effortlessly, he took off after Dawson, breathing the fresh mountain air deep into his lungs. The trails seemed barely touched and freshly groomed—like corduroy, as shredders liked to say.

Picking up speed, Pacey linked effortlessly, his fast and smooth style making even patterns in the snow. "Wahoo!" he called as he passed Dawson by.

He sped down the mountain, mostly carving and gliding. Pacey was saving the hot-dog stuff for the half-pipe or girls—whichever came first.

When they reached the bottom of the mountain,

Dawson edged to a stop right in front of Pacey, who waited by the lift line. The lines were certainly getting longer. He thought maybe they should get another long run in while they could.

Pacey gave Dawson a high-five. "You're doing great! Like a pro!" he encouraged.

"Thanks," Dawson answered. "I'm no Pacey Witter on a board, but I'm doing the best I can."

Pacey laughed, then stopped when he noticed a group of girls with boards getting into line. "Let's get in line," he urged Dawson. "Hurry!"

"What's the rush?" Dawson asked.

Pacey indicated the group of girls, and Dawson nodded knowingly. Without another word he followed Pacey through the thin red ropes into the lane where the four girls stood.

"I don't know if you've been up yet, but we just had a sick run," Pacey opened, removing his sunglasses and giving the girls a dazzling smile.

"We just got here," a petite blonde answered, as the rest of her friends turned around and took notice of Pacey and Dawson.

"It's rad up there," Pacey went on. "I'm telling you."

"Cool," a tall brunette said. "Where are you guys from?"

"Massachusetts," Dawson jumped in. "I'm Dawson, and this is Pacey."

"I'm Carla, this is Suki, that's JoAnne, and she's Fran," the blonde answered. "We're from Connecticut."

Pacey nodded. "What part of—" he started to ask, when his eyes widened in horror. Speeding toward him, at breakneck speed, was a purple blur.

And it didn't seem to have any intention of stopping.

Before Pacey could think of what to do, the blur broke right through the red ropes, crashing into him.

Pacey barely knew what hit him as he tried to untangle his neon-green arms from a pair of shocking purple legs.

"I am so sorry," he heard a voice apologize, then he figured out that he'd been hit by a girl. An out-of-control purple-wearing girl had wiped-out and plowed him over in the process.

Then Dawson's voice came at him. "Are you okay? Are either of you hurt?"

"I think I'll be all right," the girl answered, then directed a question to Pacey. "Are you okay?"

Pacey just nodded dumbly. He was too angry to say anything. The four cute girls in line in front of him giggled and whispered, before moving up toward the chairs.

Just when he had a great rap going, this tornado of a klutz had to ruin it. "You were out of control!" he finally burst as he scrambled to his feet.

"I know," the girl said sheepishly as Dawson helped her stand. "I'm a beginner. I don't know what I'm doing and now I'm going to give it a rest for a little while." Her face was beet-red, and Pacey didn't know if it was from the embarrassment or burying her face in the snow. He noticed that her hair was also red—a dark auburn tied back in a tight ponytail—a few shades darker than her face.

"Can I make it up to you somehow?" the girl asked sweetly.

"Forget it," Pacey grumbled, as he watched the Shred Bettys mount the lift ahead of him.

"Well, I'll see you around," the girl said bashfully.

"I sure hope not," Pacey muttered, as she rode away toward the lodge.

"You sure you're all right?" Dawson asked as they inched their way back into the lift line. "That was some collision!"

"Save the humiliation, I guess I'll live," Pacey muttered. "Did you see the way those girls were laughing at me?"

"Means they're not worth it," Dawson said. "They could have at least seen if you were okay."

"Or at least taken some pity on me," Pacey added. He shook his head, ready to get back on the slopes. He sure hoped he'd catch a rap with some other girls. If that clumsy redhead would stay out of his way.

Jen swept down the slope and threw her skis to a side stop at the bottom. She glanced at her watch. It was eleven-thirty. Time to get Joey.

Although the skiing was excellent, she'd had a lonely morning. She never ran into Dawson and Pacey, she didn't find anyone interesting to hook up with, and she rode every chair lift with a silent stranger.

Joey was so lucky to be getting lessons from that babe of a guy, Stinky. She wondered how Joey fared.

As she glided toward the bunny hill, Jen could see Joey and Stinky make a slow run down the hill. Joey was smiling and laughing, and she was snowplowing easily. Jen was amazed at how much progress she had made in just a few hours.

"Hey!" Jen called from the top of the hill.

Joey waved up at her, a huge smile still plastered on her face. She and Stinky grabbed hold of a small towrope that tugged them up to her.

"You look great!" Jen told Joey.

"Thanks to Stinky," Joey said with a giddy giggle. "I'll catch you later at the lodge," she told him, giving him a wave goodbye as he popped off his skis and trotted away.

"Excellent!" Stinky called. "Later!"

"Later? At the lodge? Do tell!" Jen prodded.

Joey beamed. "He's going to hang with us later." She turned thoughtful for a second. "On second thought, maybe I should hang with him, you know, separate from our group. It might not be a good idea in front of Dawson, after last night and everything . . ."

Jen nodded. "Better safe than sorry, that's my motto. So I suppose you had a good day?"

"Amazing," Joey said. "Stinky's a really good teacher. I feel comfortable on skis now. Plus, he's a total hottie."

"I noticed," Jen agreed. She glanced at her watch again. "Do you want to grab lunch now or take a run on the green trail with me?"

"I think I'm ready for a green, as long as we go slow," Joey answered.

Jen led Joey to a nearby lift. She knew that this particular one had two spots to disembark. The beginners got off at the first plateau; intermediate skiers and experts could stay on and continue riding to the top.

They were standing on line for a minute when Jen felt a presence behind her.

"Hello?" Jen heard a tentative, deep, accented voice say. "I'm sorry, but do you know what time it is?"

Jen whirled around, only to end up face-to-face with a tall, dark, handsome, blue-eyed hunk. He brushed his loose, dark curls away from his aquamarine eyes.

"It's twenty to twelve," Joey said, before Jen could answer.

"Thank you," he said, smiling broadly. "I am Jean-Pierre Mouly."

Jen was finally able to find her tongue. "Jen Lindley. And this is Joey Potter."

Jean-Pierre nodded at Jen, but continued to smile a dazzling white smile at Joey. "Joey. That is an interesting name for a girl, no?"

"It's short for Josephine," Joey explained. "But I like Joey better."

"Ah, but Josephine is a beautiful name, for a beautiful girl," Jean-Pierre said, as Joey blushed and giggled.

"Jen is short for Jennifer," Jen said, hoping that Jean-Pierre would tear his eyes away from Joey for a second.

"Yes," he said vaguely, paying as little attention as possible to Jen.

What in the world was going on? Jen thought. First, this guy Stinky falls all over Joey, and now this guy was practically swooning.

"Where are you from?" Joey asked. "I like your accent," she added with a bat of her eyelashes.

Jen felt sick. What was with Joey acting all flirty? It was so unlike her. It was discombobulating.

"I am from Montreal, Quebec," he said. "I am here with my university ski racing team. And you?"

"Somewhere not nearly as exciting," Joey answered. "Capeside, Massachusetts."

Jean-Pierre laughed gently. "Oh, but I think that Capeside must be a wonderful place if you are there."

Jen couldn't take it anymore. "This line is so long. Maybe we could grab lunch now?" she offered.

But Jean-Pierre jumped at the opportunity to get rid of Jen like a cat pouncing on a chew-toy. "If you want to wait, Joey, I'll be happy to ski down with you."

"Thanks, but I'm a beginner," Joey said, finally seeming to back down a bit.

"No matter," Jean-Pierre said. He turned to Jen, acknowledging her for the first time. "Don't you worry. I will take good care of her."

Joey gave Jen a sheepish look. "It'll just be a few minutes. I'll meet you in the lodge when I'm done. I don't want to keep you if you're hungry."

Jen sighed. "Fine," she said curtly. "Whatever. See you in the lodge." She stepped out of line and made her way toward the lodge.

What was she, dogmeat? Jen wondered. She felt like she was in the Twilight Zone or something. Usually, guys noticed her first! Why was everybody ignoring her? And noticing Joey?

First, Dawson fawned all over Joey the whole ride

up and all of last night. Then Stinky looked like he won the lottery when he took Joey as a student. Now, this French-Canadian guy was drooling all over her. Normally, Jen would be happy for Joey, who usually wasn't so self-confident.

But now, she wasn't happy at all. She didn't like being second banana. Not one bit.

Chapter 8

"I want to see some rad aerials," Dawson called out to Pacey as he stood on the sidelines of the half-pipe. He wasn't experienced enough on the board to do these types of tricks yet, but he enjoyed watching. Some of the riders were incredible, doing things that Dawson never would have thought were possible. Others bit off more than they could chew, and fell victim to some nasty wipeouts.

As Pacey waited his turn, Dawson checked out the crowd around him. He noticed a cute girl standing a few feet away. She reminded him of Joey with her straight, brown hair and pretty brown eyes.

"Hi," Dawson said, approaching her. "You ride?"

The girl turned around scowling. Maybe this wasn't going to be as easy as he thought, Dawson realized. Even worse, maybe this girl was more like Joey than he thought.

"No," the girl answered, the scowl still on her face. "But my boyfriend does." She indicated a guy wearing a red shell in the half-pipe. "That's him. And he doesn't like when I talk to total strangers."

"Okay, then," Dawson mumbled, retreating back to his original spot, and scanning the crowd for someone else interesting.

He noticed a cool-looking, athletic blonde leaning against a snowdrift. She didn't seem to be cheering on a boyfriend. Dawson decided to saunter over and try his luck with her.

He searched his mind for a good opening line, but drew a complete blank. He couldn't think of anything good to say. What do you say to a total stranger, anyway? The "Hi, I'm Dawson" thing was just too geeky, not to mention boring. "You ride?" was also kind of lame.

"Come here often?" was like something out of a seventies porno flick. "What time is it?" might just give him a response and no invitation to converse. He could ask a question about something, but he didn't want to seem like a newbie.

He kept eyeing the blonde, getting up the nerve to go over. Finally, he casually strolled by her. "Do you know someone up there?" he asked, inwardly cringing. It was an obvious attempt to find out if she had a boyfriend.

"My cousin," the blonde answered. "He's the one in navy blue."

Dawson nodded. "Yeah. I see him. He's good. My friend is waiting to go. He should be up soon." He paused, giving the girl a wide smile. "I'm Dawson Leery," he said.

"I'm too old," the girl shot back, laughing good-naturedly while looking Dawson up and down.

Dawson was taken aback at her response. She didn't seem that much older than him at all. "Just how old do you think I am?" he asked coyly.

The girl studied Dawson once again. "Sixteen," she said. "Seventeen at the most."

"Wrong," Dawson said, feeling playful. "I'm nineteen," he lied.

"Then I'm still way too old," she said. "Listen, have fun," she added, before walking over to meet her cousin, who had just gotten off the pipe.

Dawson wasn't having any luck at all today. Depressed, he walked back over to his board and sat on it in the snow. He hated going through the meet-and-greet ritual. Once in a while, he would just love it if a girl came up to him and showed interest, introducing herself, worried about saying the right thing. But he knew better; stuff like that usually never happened to him.

That's why being with Joey was so easy. He didn't have to think up clever things to say, or worry about impressing her all the time. With Joey, Dawson could just be himself. He wished meeting total strangers would be as comfortable as a conversation with Joey.

Dawson perked up when he saw Pacey on the hit—the entrance point to the half-pipe. He pushed all thoughts of meeting girls out of his mind and focused all of his attention on Pacey.

"Go Witter!" Dawson called out to support his friend. Pacey quickly picked up momentum, as he sped from one side of the U to the other. After three times, he jumped, catching the front of the board with his hands. Dawson knew that was called a nose-grab.

"All right!" Dawson cheered, and he was truly impressed. But that was nothing. On the next lap, Pacey caught more air than before, leaping out high, spinning two full turns before a perfect landing. Dawson knew that was a difficult maneuver. "Excellent seven twenty!" he called out.

Watching Pacey, Dawson nearly forgot about his girl troubles. He was proud of his friend, who seemed so confident and skilled, so in his element right now. Most people thought Pacey was a total goof-off; Dawson knew that wasn't true. He wasn't much of a student in school, mostly because he didn't see the point. But when Pacey was interested in something, he usually went over the top giving it his all, which certainly held true for snowboarding.

Pacey continued to jump and do tail-grabs, tweaks, and more aerial turns—180s, 360s, and even another 720. Before long, though, he seemed to lose some steam. At his last trick, he dismounted the half-pipe, panting.

Pacey glided over to where Dawson was sitting. Out of breath, he plopped down in the snow next to Dawson.

"You railed!" Dawson said, grabbing his hand for a shake. "Totally railed! It was amazing to watch."

"Thanks," Pacey answered, grinning. "It felt great, but I am a little out of practice."

"You didn't look it at all," Dawson assured him.

"I'm sure to be sore tomorrow," he said, sitting

up. Pacey searched the crowd. "Any good spectators?" he asked.

"Nah," Dawson said, discouraged. "I tried to
catch two raps and was shot down both times
immediately."

"Too bad," Pacey responded, shaking his head.
"Maybe we'll have better luck in the lodge."

"Speaking of which," Dawson said, glancing at
his watch. "If we want to get one more run in, now's
the time. The lifts are going to close soon."

Pacey lifted himself up, brushing the snow from
his pants. "Let's do it, then. I've got a few more
in me."

Dawson quickly got up, clamped his boots to his
board, and followed Pacey to the nearest chair lift.

Already the lines were emptying, Dawson noted.
There was also a windy chill kicking up in the air,
now that the sun was setting. Soon, darkness would
fall, bringing bitter cold into the night.

They slid right up to the end of a very short line,
then piled onto the chairlift. Dawson felt a frigid
gust of wind hit him in the face as they were
whisked up into the air. The wind continued to
blow and grew worse as they sailed closer and
closer to the top.

They rode silently for several minutes, the fatigue
from the busy day sinking in. Pacey shivered. "I'm
glad this is the last run," he said, pulling up his
neck warmer over his face. "Can't wait to get off—
this is brutal."

"No kidding," Dawson answered. Maybe taking
one last run wasn't such a great idea, he reasoned.

But luckily, they were almost there. He could see the unloading point just a few chairs ahead.

"Top, sweet top," Pacey said. "Just a few more seconds—"

Just as soon as the words were out of Pacey's mouth, the chairlift came to a shocking and abrupt halt.

"No!" Pacey groaned, as the chair rocked back and forth and the wind assaulted them from all sides.

"What happened?" Dawson asked, peering at the chairs in front of him. They usually didn't stop the chairlift—unless someone fell and was majorly blocking the way.

Dawson craned his neck a little more, and he could just see what was happening. It did look as if someone had fallen and was tangled in the chair. In fact, the purple arms and legs looked a little familiar.

"Oh no! Not again!" Pacey cried, discovering the purple blur at the same time. "It's that girl! The redhead who crashed into me! Again!"

Dawson couldn't help but chuckle. This girl was like a black cat constantly crossing their path.

Somehow, he knew that they hadn't seen the last of her.

Chapter 9

"**H**ow was your ski?" Jen asked Joey as they took a seat at the Snowbound Pub in the base lodge. They had missed each other at lunch earlier and didn't hook up for the afternoon.

"It was great," Joey said. "Jean-Pierre is a babe, huh?"

Jen nodded, but didn't say a word.

Joey couldn't believe her luck today: two gorgeous guys. On the chairlift, she had chatted with Jean-Pierre about Montreal and his racing team. Actually, she didn't do much of the talking, because she was a little freaked out about how high the chair was going. It was her first time on an actual chairlift, but thanks to Jean-Pierre's bantering, Joey was able to focus on him and not so much on the dizzying heights they were reaching.

Then they had a slow but pleasant ski down the

mountain. Though they had gone up so high, the easy trail down was pretty flat, traversing across and down the mountain in wide arcs.

Joey was so proud when they reached the bottom. She didn't even take a spill, thankfully. She didn't know if she would be able to deal with the embarrassment factor falling in front of a cute guy.

"He invited me to lunch tomorrow, and then to watch his race," Joey informed Jen.

"Good for you," Jen muttered sorely as a waitress came by and dropped off two hot chocolates that Jen had ordered while she was waiting.

Joey was taken aback by Jen's reaction. Earlier, she wanted to know all the details about Stinky. Now, she seemed sulky and uninterested in Jean-Pierre. What had gotten into her all of a sudden?

Joey didn't dwell on Jen's mood and took a sip of her delicious, milky hot chocolate. She had such a good day, and she didn't mind spending the afternoon on her own. It was kind of nice, actually. She had grabbed a quick bowl of soup for lunch, then spent some more time practicing on the bunny hill before she went up for a few more slow runs on the easy trail up the mountain. The hours flew by.

"Did you meet anyone else while you were skiing this afternoon?" Jen asked, with a trace of what sounded like bitterness to Joey.

Joey shook her head and took a sip of her hot chocolate. She was starting to get an idea of what kind bug crawled up Jen's butt. The jealousy bug.

Even though Jen was her friend, Joey smiled inside. It was about time the tables were turned. When Jen had moved to Capeside, practically everyone in town made a big fuss over her. Dawson had nearly forgotten that Joey even existed.

Now, it was nice to be the center of attention. Joey wasn't used to it; but she was loving every minute of it.

"There's Smelly," Jen pointed out.

"Stinky," Joey corrected, seeing his familiar yellow staff jacket at the pub's entrance.

"Whatever," Jen went on. "I thought you were going to meet him somewhere else, for Dawson's sake."

Joey shook her head. "I didn't get a chance to catch him to change plans," she said as she waved Stinky over. "Besides, Dawson has to get used to the fact that I might be with other guys. Plus, he's just going to hang for a little while because he has to help close up the rental shop."

"Okay," Jen said irritably. "I was just asking."

"Hey!" Stinky said, sliding into a chair next to Joey. "How'd it go for the rest of the day?"

"I think I did great!" Joey answered enthusiastically. "Of course it's because I had an excellent teacher."

"Thanks," Stinky said proudly, his dimples standing out under his five o'clock shadow. "It's my first year as an instructor, and so far I've been receiving great feedback. Excellent evaluations."

"That's terrific," Joey answered, and she was happy for him. He had demystified the whole skiing experience for her.

"In fact, if I get enough 'Excellents,' they'll consider me for a promotion next season," he continued.

"Great," Joey commented. She liked a man with ambition. "Did you want a hot chocolate or anything?" she asked.

Stinky shook his head. "Unfortunately I can't hang out. They're short staffed at the rental shop and they're in the middle of ski-return blitz. But I just wanted to stop by and say hi, and also ask you what you were doing for dinner tonight?"

"We were going to cook—" Jen started.

"I don't have any plans at all," Joey interrupted.

"Do you know the Silo? We can grab a couple of burgers there. It's fun," he offered. "Around eight?"

Joey beamed. "Sounds great."

"See you there," Stinky said, before standing and sauntering out the door.

Joey continued grinning even after he left. He was so cute; he seemed to leave a bright ember glowing in the room even when he wasn't in it anymore.

Joey took another sip of her hot chocolate, feeling warm all over. She was excited to have plans tonight, happy to get out and away from any chance of playing that stupid game again.

"Where in the world are Pacey and Dawson?" Jen asked impatiently, cutting into Joey's daydream.

Joey shrugged. "Maybe they got lucky."

Jen gave Joey an aggravated look. "So, dinner tonight with Smelly, and lunch tomorrow with Frenchie. You certainly have a busy schedule."

"Yes," Joey answered with a giggle. "Who would have guessed that I would meet two cool guys?"

"I just hope you don't get fat, you know, from all the free meals," Jen said, a pout in her voice.

Joey laughed her insult off. No stranger to bouts

of jealousy, she knew what Jen was going through. It stunk being second banana, she knew. It was no-where near as exciting as being top tomato.

Pacey stepped into the lodge, practically dragging his feet from exhaustion. He couldn't wait to sit down and sip on a nice, steaming hot chocolate. He and Dawson had nearly frozen to death when they were stuck on the chair lift because of that spastic girl. Now, he wanted to stay inside, away from the stinging wind.

He and Dawson immediately found the pub. There was a mob of people waiting for a table. Pacey silently prayed that the girls had one already.

He was in luck. Stepping into the pub, he spotted Jen and Joey right away. And to his glee, he saw they were sitting right next to the fireplace.

Pacey and Dawson pushed their way through the crowd and plopped down in the two empty seats that the girls had saved for them.

"Where have you guys been?" Jen asked testily.

"Yeah," Joey added. "Did you get lucky or something?"

Pacey shook his head sadly. "Unlucky is more like it. We were stuck on a chairlift, on the windiest part of the mountain, because of some stupid girl who fell and got caught in the chair. Plus, I think my pants are too baggy—they hide my above-average butt. Next time, I know to go tight."

Joey laughed at his joke. That was odd, Pacey thought. Usually, Joey would jump at an opportunity like that to take him down a few notches.

"Did you guys have a good day?" Dawson asked as Pacey tried to get the waitress's attention.

Joey and Jen responded at the same time.

"It was okay," Jen answered listlessly.

"It was great!" was Joey's hearty reply.

Pacey cocked an eyebrow at Dawson. There was certainly something weird going on between those two. He was just about to find out what when he felt something pour down his back.

Something wet and extremely hot.

Something that smelled like scalding, black coffee.

"Aaahh!" Pacey screamed, jumping up.

Searching the faces of his friends, Pacey knew what had just happened. Someone had spilled coffee on him.

And he didn't even need to turn around to see who it was.

Chapter 10

"**W**hat is wrong with you!" Pacey shouted, as he whirled around.

Dawson couldn't believe Pacey's outburst. Usually he didn't have such a bad temper.

But sure enough, the klutzy redheaded girl was right behind him, holding an empty coffee cup. "I—I—I'm so sorry!" she said. "I just came over to apologize again for running into you this morning. I can't believe I spilled my—"

"Well I can believe it!" Pacey exploded. "First, you nearly flatten me on the lift line. Then, I nearly freeze to death when you fall on the lift. Now, I have third-degree burns because of your clumsy, dumb luck!"

Dawson's heart went out to the girl as he saw her horrified expression and face grow red. She looked like she was on the verge of tears.

"Look," Dawson said, trying to calm Pacey down. He felt so badly for this girl, even though she was definitely a klutz. "She didn't mean it. It wasn't her fault."

Pacey scowled and flopped back down in his seat. He let out an angry breath. "Just do me a favor," he said, shooting the girl an angry glare. "Stay as far away from me as possible."

The redheaded girl nodded, not uttering another sound. Then, with her head hanging low, she slowly slunk away.

"Who was that?" Joey asked.

"You don't want to know," Pacey answered grimly.

Dawson figured that now would be a good time to lighten the mood and change the subject. "Pacey was great on the half-pipe today. You guys should have seen him," he said, saying the first thing that entered his mind.

But he got no response; Jen grumbled, Pacey stewed, and Joey seemed off in another world.

Dawson sighed, wondering if he should try again.

He didn't have to. Right at that moment, a bearded man stepped on stage and took the microphone. He greeted the crowd heartily. "Good evening snow enthusiasts!" he said. "Now's the time you've all been waiting for."

Dawson noticed that his friends finally started to perk up with interest.

"I am proud to present, back by popular demand, the sweet sounds of my own daughter," the man went on. "Ladies and Gentlemen, please welcome the Snowbound Pub's own Kyra Wolfson."

The crowd applauded, when a familiar figure took the stage, and sat on a stool with her guitar.

Dawson turned to Pacey. He couldn't believe what he saw.

Pacey, wide-eyed, returned his glance.

Dawson couldn't help but laugh. There, on stage, was the clumsy redhead.

"It's not funny," Pacey said irritably. "She's bound to hit a wrong note and start an avalanche. Or maybe she'll fall off the stage, knock over a lamp, and start a fire. Where is the nearest exit by the way?"

Jen hushed him. "Ssh! I want to hear her."

Kyra cleared her throat and gave the crowd a shy smile before she began. Dawson thought she looked different, now that she had changed from her purple ski-outfit into a black turtleneck and faded jeans that clung to her curves. And her hair was no longer tied back; it hung generously down around her shoulders, shining rainbow colors in the stage lights. Her green eyes stood out like emeralds against the vibrant auburn of her hair and the porcelain pureness of her skin.

She led into Jewel's "I Was Meant for You," singing so sweetly that when Dawson closed his eyes he thought it was Jewel herself.

Dawson turned to Pacey again. "She's amazing!" he said, but Pacey didn't hear him. Much to Dawson's amusement, Pacey's eyes were transfixed on the stage, his mouth agape in . . . Dawson couldn't quite figure out what. Was it shock? Admiration?

Dawson poked Pacey in the elbow. "She's terrific, huh?"

Pacey emerged from his zombielike state. "She's . . . she's . . . Did she look that cute on the mountain today?"

That was the answer, Dawson realized. He could easily read Pacey's expression now: astonished lust.

The crowd cheered when Kyra finished her set with a Shawn Colvin tune. Pacey clapped and whistled boisterously.

"Isn't that the girl whose head you just bit off?" Joey asked, applauding also.

"Um, yeah . . ." Pacey admitted. "But I was just joking. Do you think I was too harsh?"

"Harsh is nothing compared to the way you acted toward her," Jen admonished.

Pacey wished more than anything that he could turn back time, and change what had happened. Miraculously, the cloddish redheaded clown from the slopes was anything but all thumbs on the guitar. And she was simply . . . beautiful. Pacey was kicking himself for not noticing that before.

How could he have been such a jerk? Her clumsiness was the perfect opportunity for a rap! Didn't she even offer to make it up to him earlier? If he could relive the day, Pacey would accept the offer in a split second.

He couldn't take his eyes off of her. Kyra—what a beautiful and interesting name. There had to be a way for him to get to know her better. *If* she would ever speak to him again, after the way he yelled at her like an idiot.

Pacey stood when he saw Kyra step off the stage.

He had to apologize to her. He just hoped she wouldn't crack the guitar over his head.

"You're not—" Dawson said, catching the determined look in Pacey's eye.

"I am," Pacey countered. "I have to."

Pacey strode away from the table, approaching Kyra as she crouched down and packed up her equipment.

"That was a great set," Pacey said kindly.

Kyra looked up, startled. "Oh it's you," she said dryly. "Don't worry, I'm getting out of here in a second," she added as she snapped her guitar case shut. She stood up to leave, but Pacey caught her gently by the arm.

"Listen, I'm sorry for yelling before," Pacey said. He mustered a feeble excuse. "I had a bad day today. Please accept my apology. In fact, I won't leave here until you forgive me."

Kyra stood and a slow smile crept across her face. "Okay," she said uncertainly. "I shouldn't make it so easy but . . . your apology is accepted. But only if you'll accept mine."

"Already done. My name is Pacey Witter, and I am now your biggest fan. I would be honored if you let me take you to dinner tonight to make up for my rude, boorish behavior," he gallantly offered.

"Kyra Wolfson," she said, shaking Pacey's extended hand. "If joining you atones for my clumsiness, it's a deal. It's just that I get really nervous around cute guys," she added shyly.

Pacey couldn't believe his luck. What was it about him that attracted clumsy women? he thought. First Andie and now Kyra. Kyra thought he was cute?

Maybe that was why she seemed to be around him all day. "Great!" he said happily. "Um, I don't really know the area that well. But I'd like to take you somewhere nice—"

"Paulo's Pizza will be fine with me," she cut in, her green eyes sparkling. "It's near my home. Why don't you meet me there around eight o' clock?"

"All right, then," he responded, his chest filling with glee. "See you at eight."

When he turned to rejoin his friends, Kyra called after him. "I'd wear old clothes, if I were you," she said. "I've been known to spill things."

Pacey laughed and gave her the thumbs up. He felt like skipping back to the table. When he approached Dawson, he held out his hand for a high-five.

"No way," Dawson said incredulously. "I can't believe she even looked at you."

"Finally, finally, I got lucky!" Pacey enthused, as he plopped down next to his buddy. "Who would have guessed that the girl of my dreams was right under my nose the whole day. I'm taking her out to dinner tonight!"

"Good going," Dawson said.

"I guess that leaves just you and me dateless for tonight," Jen said glumly.

"You got lucky, too?" Pacey asked Joey. "There are more desperate guys out there than I thought."

"I guess there are," Joey said, not giving any further information.

Pacey could see Dawson's wounded expression. But Dawson seemed to steel himself, asking very calmly. "That's great. Who's the lucky guy?"

"Guys," Jen corrected. "Plural. Her ski instructor is taking her to dinner tonight, then a French-Canadian ski-racer is buying her lunch tomorrow."

Joey shot Jen a sharp glance, then looked down at the table, obviously uncomfortable.

"Two dates," Dawson said, making a huge effort to be cool. "That's terrific, Joey. Have a great time."

"Thanks," Joey answered genuinely.

Pacey suddenly wished Dawson would meet someone. But, even though he hadn't, Pacey had to hand it to him—Dawson was handling the situation incredibly well.

Finally, the weekend was shaping up the way Pacey had hoped. He was happy with his performance on the slopes today. Dawson hadn't moaned about Joey once the whole day. And, most importantly, he had a date with the most beautiful, talented girl he had ever met.

Chapter 11

"**F**ull house," Jen said triumphantly, placing her cards on the table. "That means I win."

"I know what it means," Dawson answered, as he pulled out his wallet. "How much do I owe you?"

"Five big ones," Jen said, holding out her palm. "If you're going to swim with the sharks you have to pay the consequences."

Dawson mock-reluctantly handed the money over. "How did you learn to play poker so well, anyway?"

Jen laughed. "My grandmother on my father's side taught me. She had a great gaming spirit. She was the complete opposite of Grams."

Jen was having a great time lazily playing cards with Dawson. The house was so cozy and peaceful without Joey and Pacey. It was so quiet, they could hear the high-pitched whistle of the wind outside over the crackle of the fire.

While Joey was busy meeting new guys, Jen figured she could take care of the home front: specifically Dawson. When she first realized she'd be home alone with him all night, Jen had visions of wearing something sexy and seducing him under the spell of the roaring fire. But she felt so comfortable with Dawson just then she thought she'd try a subtler bewitchment.

When they had come back from the slopes earlier, Jen was grouchy and tired. She took a nap and now felt like a whole new person. She realized how ornery she had acted at the pub. And she knew that sulking because Joey was being showered with male attention wasn't going to get her anywhere.

She decided that if she wanted a guy to notice her she had to be proactive, and in the case of Dawson, that would include companionship and a dazzling home-cooked meal.

"Should I deal another hand?" Dawson asked.

Jen glanced at her wristwatch. "It's getting kind of late." She didn't start dinner until later because they were having so much fun playing cards. "I should check on the chicken parm."

"That reminds me," Dawson said, smiling. "I'm starving. And it smells awfully good."

"It should be done any minute," Jen said, rising to move to the kitchen.

"I'll set the table," Dawson offered as he followed her.

Jen was surprised at how light Dawson's mood was even though Joey was on a date. She was glad—operation "win back Dawson" would be much harder if he were moping about Joey all night.

Dawson opened a cabinet and took out some dishes. "Hey!" he exclaimed. "There's some cookbooks in here if we want to get creative tomorrow night."

Jen pulled the chicken parm out of the oven and placed the pan on a hot plate. "Cookbooks?" Jen repeated. "That's strange. My mom doesn't cook at all."

"Looks like she decided to take it up," Dawson said, peering at the titles on the spines. "Dinners for Two. Candlelight Cuisine. Leftovers for Lovers."

Jen felt a pang in her chest. Wiping her hands with the dishtowel, she walked over to look over Dawson's shoulders. "Let me see those," she demanded.

Dawson pulled them out of the cupboard and placed each book on the counter. Jen immediately opened one. On the title page, an inscription in jumped out at her. She didn't recognize the flowery handwriting; it certainly wasn't her mother's. It read: *To my love, so I may feed your hunger in our winter hideaway love nest. Sharon.*

"Sharon?" Jen read out loud. "Who the hell is she?"

Her hands started to shake as she slammed the book shut. Suddenly, things started to fall into place. The "adult" games. The slinky clothes in the closet. The cookbooks. "Hideaway lovenest." It all could only mean one thing.

Her father was having an affair. With some tart, right here, in the Lindley family cabin.

Her breath grew short, and a well of tears filled

Jen's eyes. An anguished sob escaped from deep inside her.

"What's the matter?" Dawson asked, a look of shock on his face.

Jen wanted to tell him, but she couldn't speak right then. Another sob came out of her throat.

She had to lie down. Jen felt a little dizzy and nauseous all of a sudden. She raced to the family room and threw herself on the couch.

The tears flowed freely now, and Jen didn't know if she ever would be able to stop crying.

She felt Dawson sit next to her. He gently reached out an arm and pulled her up to him. The next thing she knew, Jen buried her face into Dawson's chest, clinging to him for her dear life, her tears dripping down his shirt.

"Shhh," Dawson soothed. "It's okay. Tell me what's the matter. It will make you feel better."

Finally, Jen took a deep breath. "I told you my mother doesn't cook. Did you see that inscription? Hideaway lovenest?"

Dawson nodded, the realization dawning on him.

"My father must be having an affair. This is his 'hideaway lovenest' with his mistress," Jen was able to choke out before tears threatened to return. "In the very same cabin he shared with his family. How disgusting!" she fumed.

"You don't know that for sure," Dawson said, trying his best to comfort her. "For all you know they could have bought those books at a garage sale. It's circumstantial evidence."

Jen shook her head. "He probably thinks I'm as deaf, dumb, and blind as my mother," she insisted, her eyes tearing up all over again. "I found these nighties and sexy clothes in the closet upstairs. They're two sizes smaller than my mom. And how do you explain those games we found: Foreplay, Touch and Tickle? Is that all circumstantial, too?"

Jen could tell Dawson didn't know what to say. He drew her tighter in his arms as she went on. "And that explains the way my father said that the cabin should he "all clear" this weekend. Why wouldn't it be? My parents haven't come up here in ages. But *he* has! When he's on one of his 'business trips' he must be frolicking up here."

Dawson let out a breath, giving Jen another reassuring squeeze. "I'm sorry, Jen. I know exactly what you're going through. When I found out my mom was having an affair . . . my whole world came crashing down."

"My parents' marriage has been far from perfect, you know?" Jen reflected. "But I just never expected . . . right in my face!"

"I understand," Dawson said quietly. "All too well."

They sat in silence while the fire crackled in front of them, casting shadows on their faces. Jen was furious at her dad right then, not only for cheating on her mom, but for ruining her night. The chicken parm was sure to be cold by now, and any hopes of charming Dawson were lost. She wasn't in the mood.

"What ever happened to commitment?" Jen asked, breaking the quiet. "Why don't people take marriage seriously anymore? When I get married, I'm going to follow the vows to the letter."

"Or else why bother?" Dawson finished, his face growing sad with painful memories. "I don't understand why if you love someone enough to say you're going to spend the rest of your life with them, why you would ever want to jeopardize it." He drew in a deep breath. "My mother tried to explain it to me a thousand times. She insists that she loves my dad more than anyone in the world. I still don't get why she cheated on him then."

Jen shook her head, and dabbed at her puffy eyes with her shirt. "Parents are such hypocrites. They sent me away because they thought I was growing up too fast. Well, maybe I was. But at least I could say that I never cheated on any of my boyfriends."

She looked right into Dawson's handsome face right then, his sympathetic brown eyes warming her heart. Right then, it felt so good to be in his arms. She was so happy to have his comfort.

She turned her face up toward his, opening her mouth to thank him. But before she knew it, Dawson's mouth was on hers.

She hadn't planned on seducing Dawson this way. But as Jen drank in Dawson's caring kisses, her troubles, for the moment, seemed to fade away.

Pacey nervously waited at the corner table in Paolo's Pizza. He drummed his fingers on the red-and-white-checkered tablecloth. Glancing at his watch for what seemed like the hundredth time, he saw that it was five minutes after eight. Pacey prayed that he wasn't going to be stood up.

But who could blame Kyra if she did stand him up? He acted like the biggest jerk to her, screaming at her in the middle of the pub like that. It would serve him right if she left him sitting there like a loser.

Pacey figured he'd give her ten more minutes, then he'd start panicking. He studied the photos on the wall next to him to kill time. Paolo's was a cute, festive little place. Pictures of laughing families, smiling couples, and the owners and waitstaff posing with celebrities covered every inch of one wall. Another wall displayed the Roman Coliseum, while the opposite one exhibited the Leaning Tower of Pisa. The waitstaff bustled past with large trays full of mouth-watering pizzas and tasty-looking pastas.

Finally, the glass door opened and Pacey could see Kyra step inside.

"Bellissima," a waiter shouted when he saw her.

"Hey, Giuseppe," she said, as she unzipped her winter jacket and hung it from a peg on the wall. She waved at the other waiters, too. It seemed like she was a favorite customer.

Pacey stood up from his seat, straightening his red bowling shirt as she walked over. Suddenly, he wished he had worn something dressier: Kyra looked stunning in a kelly-green turtleneck and a short black miniskirt. But Pacey could tell by Kyra's easy smile that his style suited her just fine.

"Hello," Pacey greeted, admiring the way her turtleneck matched her dancing eyes. He scooted over to her side of the table and pulled out the chair for her.

"Thank you," Kyra said as she sat. "So, what do you think of the place?" she asked.

"I like it," Pacey said, glancing around and nodding. "It's just my speed and it seems fun."

"You have no idea how fun it can get in here," Kyra said laughing. "Just you wait."

A waiter placed two menus in front of them, then whisked off to help another table. "The food is great. They have great pasta in addition to the pizza," Kyra pointed out. "But my mom and I are huge fans of the pizza here. We come here and order the same pie, at least once a week."

"Pepperoni and mushroom," the waiter said as he paused at the table. "Coming right up?"

Kyra giggled. "See? I don't even have to order. But I'll be happy to get something else tonight . . ."

The waiter turned to Pacey with arched eyebrows. "One pepperoni and mushroom pie sounds great to me," he said, clapping the menu shut.

"Excellent choice, sir," the waiter said as he collected the menus and swept away to put the order in.

Pacey leaned across the table, smiling at Kyra. "So," he said, picking up a spoon and speaking into it like a microphone. "Tell me about the mysterious and clumsy, but beautiful, Kyra Wolfson." He held the spoon by her mouth as if he was a reporter vying for the scoop.

"Well, I've never been very graceful," Kyra started, blushing. "But I'm not always like today. Today was my first time on a snowboard—I'm much more of a skier," she added.

"I sure hope so," Pacey said, placing the spoon on the table. He adored the musical quality of her laugh.

"I thought if you could ski, then snowboarding was a no-brainer," she admitted sheepishly. "Boy, was I wrong!"

"Have you thought of taking lessons?" Pacey asked.

"Now I'm thinking about it," Kyra said.

"What are you doing tomorrow?" Pacey asked, sensing an opportunity.

"Not much," Kyra answered, "I was thinking about terrorizing the mountain again. But I'm not so sure . . ."

Pacey grinned. "I can give you lessons. Make you less of a menace to society."

Kyra's eyes widened. "That would be great," she said as a waiter slammed down a pitcher of soda on their table. Then she added shyly, "I noticed how good you were, out on the slopes."

"Thanks," Pacey said, happily surprised. Kyra must have had her sights set on him all day! And he was too dumb to realize it.

He poured some soda for her and then a glass for himself. Raising a glass in a cheer, he said, "So I assume you live right here in Steep Mountain. You mentioned this place was near your house."

Kyra nodded as she took a sip of soda. "My parents and I moved here six years ago from New Jersey. Mom and Dad wanted to get away from it all—the crowds, the congestion. She left her job at a brokerage house, they bought the Snowbound Pub, and the rest is history."

Pacey adored her chatty, personable manner. He felt an instant intimacy with her. "Have you always sung at the pub?" he wanted to know.

Kyra shook her head. "I just got up the nerve to do it this year. I'm in a choir in my high school—I'm a sophomore—and Dad taught me how to play guitar. My parents always encouraged me to perform, and I finally took them up on their challenge this past December." She punctuated the last sentence with a laugh. "And now I can't get enough! You need a hook to get me off the stage!" Kyra paused, brushing a strand of hair out of her face. "Enough about me. What about you?" she asked Pacey.

Pacey told her all about Capeside, making some all-too-true jokes about his dysfunctional family. He told her about how for fun he enjoyed playing basketball, hanging out with his friends, and entering beauty pageants.

"It's true!" Pacey told her. "Though I only did it once, so I could win enough money to move out of my house. Unfortunately, I lost."

Kyra laughed, and she seemed to enjoy every one of Pacey's wacky stories. "I think that took a lot of guts!" she complimented.

"Well, my dad scaled me like a fish when I got home. So I don't how many 'guts' are actually left," he said.

Kyra's expression turned tender for a moment. "I think you still have guts. It took a lot of guts for you to come and apologize to me."

Pacey disagreed. "That was human decency. Not guts. But maybe I'll grow some more of both traits one of these days."

Kyra seemed so interested in everything Pacey had to say. Pacey wasn't used to that, especially coming from his large family where he could barely get a word in edgewise among all the yelling.

When the pizza came, Pacey and Kyra shared it in silence with another pitcher of soda. It struck Pacey that on a first date, he usually felt awkward during the silences. But with Kyra, it was different. Just being with her was so easy; so natural and comfortable, like he'd known her forever.

As they ate, a tuxedoed gentleman approached the table. "We're in for a treat now," Kyra whispered, smiling up at the man.

The man brushed off his velvet tuxedo jacket and snapped his fingers. *"Volare! Whoa-oh!"* he belted out. The whole restaurant clapped along as he continued to sing, strolling and stopping at tables along the way.

Pacey and Kyra laughed. Pacey thought the guy had a good voice, but his manner was so smarmy, like some kind of lounge-singing character on *Saturday Night Live*, complete with thick gold necklaces, pinky rings, and a ruffled tuxedo shirt unbuttoned to his waist.

When the singer finished, everyone cheered, and the gentleman took a bow. Then he started another tune: *"When the moon hits the sky like a big pizza pie, that's amore . . ."* he crooned. He waved his hands in the air, gesturing everyone to sing along.

Pacey lifted his soda glass and swayed it as he joined in. "That's amore!" he sang. He knew he didn't have much of a singing voice, but he was having so much fun, he didn't care. "That's amore!"

Kyra leaned toward Pacey. "How about I swap

some singing lessons for the snowboard lessons?" she asked above the din.

Pacey smiled. "You've got a deal!" he agreed. Taking a hearty bite out of his pepperoni and mushroom slice, he suddenly felt like all of his senses came alive. Everything around him looked colorful and festive and beautiful—especially Kyra. He thought he had never heard such a sweet sound as her voice, humming along with an old Sinatra tune the entertainer was now bellowing.

Impulsively, Pacey took Kyra's hand, giving it a gentle squeeze. Kyra was right. He never imagined how much fun a simple pizza place could be. And tonight, he was having the time of his life.

Chapter 12

"That was when I saved a life right on the slopes," Stinky said, as Joey stifled a yawn. "Did I tell you about that?"

"Twice," Joey said, a little too harshly. Noticing Stinky's hurt look she quickly added, "But both times it was a great story."

Joey felt trapped in Stinky's car. She wanted to get out so she could crawl into bed and crash. She was exhausted from skiing all day, but not as tired as she was hearing Stinky talk about himself.

Joey didn't realize that a conversation didn't necessarily need two people. It was also amazing, she thought, that at the end of the night, Stinky didn't know anything about her except for her name. It was like he was trying to get some kind of special award for not asking her one single question all night.

"Well," Joey cut in on a monologue about mountains he'd skied. She placed her hand on the door handle. "If I'm going to make my lesson early, I'll have to get to bed early."

"Oh, okay," Stinky said, seeming disappointed. "We can continue our conversation tomorrow," he said. He leaned over and gave Joey a peck on the cheek, which she was actually able to accept without cringing. "And don't forget, you have to fill out the evaluation form tomorrow after the lesson's over."

"Okay, bye, thanks for dinner," Joey said, practically all in one breath. She stepped out of the car and quickly shut the door. It was amazing what good looks did to some guys, she thought.

Stepping up onto the porch, Joey turned and waved at Stinky's quick beep. Poor guy, she thought, feeling sorry for him for a split second. He actually really seemed to like her. But if she had to hear another sentence starting with "I" or if she heard "evaluation form" one more time she thought she might scream.

He was one of those to-the-max, extreme, over-achiever types. He had to excel at everything he did—and boast about it later. What struck Joey as funny was that it seemed that he was most concerned about getting a perfect score on his evaluation from her. The funny part was that he was actually a good teacher. He didn't need to worry about it so much or try so hard to ensure a good evaluation.

She slowly opened the door, taking off her boots

as she stepped inside. The house seemed eerily quiet. She figured that Dawson and Jen probably turned in early from all the exertion of a full day on the slopes.

She walked past the kitchen, carrying her boots. She stopped, noticing a pan of food sitting on the counter, cold and untouched, like someone had made it and then run out the door.

That was certainly curious. She hoped everything was okay.

Joey turned when she heard some shuffling in the family room. She stood still, silently listening for clues. There was someone in there. Maybe it was a burglar—and Jen and Dawson had run out when they heard him break in.

What should she do? Thinking quickly, Joey grabbed a copper skillet from the rack above the stove. Stealthily, she tiptoed to the family room. She flattened herself against the wall, listening.

She wasn't quite sure of the noises she was hearing. She heard the crackle of a fire and some movement. But there was more. She couldn't figure out who—or what—might be in there.

Joey took a deep breath and decided to go for it, swinging through the doorway with the skillet over head.

"Aaaaah!" she screamed, dropping the skillet to the floor.

"Aaah!" Dawson and Jen screeched, abruptly breaking a tight embrace.

Joey breathed out, putting a hand on her fast-beating heart. "I'm sorry," she said. "I thought there was—that you were—a b-b-burglar or something," she stammered, growing more and more embarrassed at their uncomfortable glances. "I saw the chicken," she started to explain, but gave it up. She composed herself. "Sorry. I'm going to bed now. Good night."

Joey went over the scene in her mind as she raced up the stairs. Dawson and Jen were liplocked, right there on the couch. That was certainly a shock to the system.

Seeing them together again sent a flood of familiar feelings racing through Joey. Reaching her bedroom, she closed the door behind her, and peeled off her clothes.

Joey tried to think back on her date to mute the tug she felt at her heart. But it wouldn't work. No matter how hard she tried, she couldn't get the image out of her mind; the image of Jen and Dawson kissing on the couch.

She didn't know why she cared so much. What else should she expect from Dawson? She just told him last night that she didn't want to get back together. And she wasn't even able to tell him if she still loved him. Not to mention that she was dating two guys in one weekend.

She didn't expect Dawson to sit around and pine for her forever. But starting things up with Jen again didn't seem like such a good idea for him.

Joey tried to shake the thought out of her mind. It was simply none of her business.

A nagging feeling covered her, like she had been

left out in the cold. She knew it was selfish and silly to feel that way. But she just couldn't help it. Why was Joey suddenly wishing to be the girl on the couch with Dawson?

Stricken, Dawson pulled away from Jen and stared hopelessly up the stairs. What bad timing. Why did Joey have to come in just then?

He didn't know how it happened. One minute, he was consoling Jen, hugging her and stroking her hair, simply to calm her. The next thing he knew they were kissing furiously. He didn't even know for how long.

"I'm sorry," Jen said softly.

Dawson sighed, turning back to her. "Why are you sorry? It wasn't your fault. I shouldn't have—I don't want you to think I was taking advantage—"

Jen shook her head. "I don't think you were taking advantage. I'm just sorry about Joey. I'm not blind. I know you're trying to get her back. I know that her seeing us upset you."

Dawson didn't know what to say. He just sat on the couch uncomfortably, stone quiet.

"It felt good, though, didn't it?" Jen said. "Like old times. This kiss now and last night's, too."

Dawson nodded. It did feel good. It felt great to hold someone; to kiss someone. He just wanted so badly for that someone to be Joey.

Joey. She had looked surprised, that was for sure. But was that a trace of disturbance he saw on her face as well?

Dawson wrinkled his brow, deep in thought.

What if that sparked a little jealousy in Joey? Would jealousy make her old feelings for him come back around?

And what if he asked Jen to ski with him tomorrow? Would that make Joey jealous, too?

He sure hoped so.

Chapter 13

"Good morning everybody! Rise and shine!" Pacey bellowed the next morning. He knew it was early, but he was excited to hit the slopes. He had made plans to meet up with Kyra at the lodge at eight o'clock sharp. If these guys weren't going to get out of bed he wasn't going to wait for them.

But he was dying to tell someone about his date. By the time he had come home last night, everyone was asleep. He was tempted to wake Dawson up last night, and rehash the night with him, but he thought better of it.

Pacey relived the end of the night in his mind. After the pizza joint, Kyra suggested that they go candlepin bowling. They had walked down the road from Paulo's to the small red barn that housed the bowling alley.

Pacey had never been candlepin bowling before,

so he didn't know what to expect. It was completely different from the bowling he knew, but just as much fun. The ball was much smaller than a regular bowling ball—like a shotput that fit snugly in his whole hand. The pins were tall and narrow—not pear shaped—and they were lighter, which meant they bounced and scattered more easily.

At first, candlepin bowling seemed like it was going to be cake to Pacey, because of the lighter, smaller ball and taller pins. But he soon found out that it wasn't as easy as it looked. Good candlepin bowlers were very precise, and it was easy to lose control with the little ball.

He and Kyra had a great time, laughing and bowling, and playing songs on the jukebox at the alley. Pacey discovered that he and Kyra had the same taste in music.

There was even a small ice cream shop right next door, and Pacey treated Kyra to a chocolate chip cookie dough cone, with ice cream that was homemade right there in Vermont.

Pacey had known it was getting late when they were eating ice cream. But he didn't want the date to end. They had hit it off fabulously, and Kyra didn't even fall, spill, or break anything the whole time. She seemed completely relaxed around Pacey, and vice versa.

Even though Pacey didn't want the night to end, he drove her home as soon as they finished their ice creams. No point in making the parental units angry by getting her home late, he figured.

She lived in a small, simple gray farmhouse, just

down the road from the pizza place. They made a plan to meet for the next day, then Pacey leaned in, and not wanting to be too forward, gave her a quick peck on the lips.

Amazingly, Kyra pulled him back, for a longer, lingering kiss that nearly knocked his socks off. Thinking about it again this morning set Pacey's heart on fire.

Pacey snapped out of his daydream and decided to do something about his three sleepyheaded friends. He took two copper skillets and banged them together.

"Morning! Breakfast!" he shouted. And before he knew it, three angry bed-headed people stormed into the kitchen.

"It's six-thirty," Joey growled. "What in the world is wrong with you."

"We should hit the slopes as early as we can. We shouldn't waste the day," Pacey explained.

"But the slopes don't open until eight o'clock," Jen croaked. "And why are you so chipper this morning?"

"Funny you should ask," Pacey said, flipping one skillet over and catching it by the handle. "It just so happens that I had an amazing, excellent, out-of-control fabulous, date last night."

"That's great," Dawson said, between yawns. "I'm really glad things went well."

Pacey nodded and smiled. "I've never met anyone like her. She's so different.

"By the way," Pacey asked, remembering Joey's date. "How did your evening go last night?"

Joey scowled, not seeming to want to talk so early

in the morning. Pacey noticed she gave Dawson and Jen an uneasy look, then muttered, "It was great. Totally great. I, too, had a night to remember."

"And what did you guys end up doing last night?" Pacey asked Dawson and Jen, who exchanged their own uneasy looks.

"We kept . . . ourselves . . . busy," Dawson said tentatively, though Pacey didn't know why. Then he changed the subject. "So, where's breakfast? That's the only reason I got out of bed."

That was a good point, Pacey realized. He hadn't quite made anything yet. "I was about to whip up a tasty, giant omelet," he said, though he had no idea how to make one. No worry, he thought. Today, he felt so great, he felt like there was nothing he couldn't do.

Dawson and Jen sat on the chairlift in silence. Dawson reflected on the night before, not sure what to say or do. Luckily, Jen was totally normal today, and Dawson was thankful for that. But he couldn't forget the look on Joey's face when she saw them kissing. But she didn't say a word this morning and made a point of telling them how successful her date was the night before.

Then he remembered how the whole thing had happened in the first place: Jen's discovery of her dad's affair. "How are you doing today?" Dawson asked awkwardly. "About your parents, I mean."

A sad expression clouded Jen's face. "Awful. I don't know what to do, either. Should I just tell Mom? Part of me is so angry with Dad that I want to. Or should I approach Dad first, and let him do it?"

Dawson nodded thoughtfully. "That's a tough question," he said. "Maybe you should confront your dad first. Your mother might be humiliated that you knew before her—take it from me."

"Good point," Jen said as she mulled over the possibilities. "I'm just so confused. I don't know what the right thing to do is. Maybe I should mind my own business and not do anything at all."

"I don't think that's a good idea," Dawson said. "It will eat at you inside. You need to unload it."

"Well, I guess I can't do anything until they get back from London anyway," Jen mused. "And I guess I should try to salvage what's left of the weekend."

Dawson lifted up the safety bar as they got ready to hop off the chairlift.

"Let's not talk about them anymore, okay?" Jen said, as she de-fogged her sunglasses.

"Whatever you want," Dawson said as he pulled out a trail map. "Just know that I'm here for you if you need to talk."

"I know you are," Jen said, a wistful tone in her voice.

Dawson's heart leaped, and he didn't know what to do. Before he got into any more trouble trying to console her, he thrust the trail map into her hands. "What about taking Bear Trap this time. It looks like it has a lot of fun moguls. And it empties out right in the main area."

Jen nodded, and they took off for the trail, Dawson on his board, Jen on her skis.

As they sailed down the mountain, Dawson noticed the beautiful, white-capped pine trees. He sucked in a breath of mountain air, so distinct from the Capeside sea breezes.

They continued down, jumping some moguls, carving around others. When the trail ended, they merged into the common area, where people in multicolored outfits dotted the slope like sprinkles on a vanilla ice cream cone.

One bright blue jacket especially stood out to Dawson. Was that Joey, slowly meandering down the hill with her instructor?

It sure was, he realized, as she passed him, completely oblivious to his presence. Dawson thought that she probably forgot all about what had happened between he and Jen last night. He desperately wanted to do something to remind her.

He stuck to the sidelines, speeding up until he was ahead of Joey. Jen kept closely behind him. *Perfect*, Dawson thought.

When they had reached just the right point, Dawson stopped abruptly. Jen stopped too.

"Something wrong?" she asked. "Why did you stop like that?"

"Just had to fix my boot," Dawson lied, bending down to fiddle with it. He furtively peered up the mountain. Joey was slowly, cluelessly, heading in their direction. Now was the time to make his move.

Playfully, Dawson gave Jen a shove, sending her tumbling to the ground. "Whoa!" she said.

Dawson scooped up a handful of snow and sprinkled it on her.

"Dawson!" Jen screeched, giggling. "Cut it out!"

"I thought you could use some cheering up," he said as he leaned over her, planting his arms on either side of her torso. He brought his face closer to her and smiled, and he fleetingly thought of kissing her again.

But that thought dissolved when he saw Joey come up behind them. "Oh, hi," Dawson said, feigning surprise.

Joey came to a slow stop, with her instructor behind her. Just as Dawson had hoped, she seemed astonished at their compromising position. "Hey," she said awkwardly. "Did you guys wipe out or something?"

Dawson rolled away from Jen and helped her up. "Just having fun. You're looking pretty good there, though, like you've learned a lot. Are you her instructor?" Dawson asked the guy she was with.

"Yes, Chad Matthews," he said, extending a gloved hand. "But you can call me Stinky."

Dawson suppressed a howl as he shook his hand. Joey was dating a guy named Stinky? "Dawson Leery," he introduced himself. "Nice to meet you. We've heard good things," he added magnanimously, chuckling at Joey's blush.

"In no time she'll be giving Pikaboo Street a run for her money," Stinky joked, putting an arm around Joey.

"Yeah," Jen said, tugging at Dawson, seemingly eager to move on. "Good seeing you guys. We'll catch you later at the races."

"Bye," Joey said, as Stinky waved them off.

Dawson followed Jen down the rest of the hill, self-satisfied. His little plan had worked perfectly.

Not only did Joey seem uncomfortable and curious about what was going on with Jen, she also seemed amazed that Dawson was acting so cool, introducing himself pleasantly to her instructor and making small talk. He hoped she would spend a good part of the day thinking it over.

Jen came to a stop in front of Dawson at the bottom. "That was a fun run," she said, her mood lightening for the first time since last night.

Suddenly, a guilty feeling enveloped Dawson. He knew he was using Jen to play games with Joey. But he wasn't doing anything harmful, was he? He and Jen had been known to goof around before, and he hadn't actually kissed her. Still, Dawson didn't want Jen to get the wrong idea.

With everything that Jen was going through right now, Dawson realized that maybe it wasn't such a good idea to lead her on in even the smallest ways.

A heavy weight started to press on Dawson's insides. He knew what he had been doing, no matter how subtly, was wrong. He had to find another way to get Joey back—without playing with the feelings of his good friend Jen.

Chapter 14

"*O*ver here, *ma chérie*," Jean-Pierre called out when Joey approached the Snowbound Pub.

Joey waved at him, struck by how gorgeous he looked. It was hard to decide who was cuter—Jean-Pierre or Stinky. Today part of her warmth for Stinky returned. When he was teaching, he was clear, clever, and thoughtful. It was when he wasn't teaching that he was a total bore.

Lucky for Stinky, Joey filled out an evaluation for his teaching skills, not his dating skills, after the lesson today. She gave him the Excellent he wanted so badly; he actually deserved it.

When she reached the table, Jean-Pierre stood, then reached out, took her hand, and kissed it. "You look *très belle* today," he said.

"*Merci*," Joey answered, flattered by his romantic, gentlemanly treatment.

"You speak French?" Jean-Pierre asked in surprise.

"*Un peu*," Joey responded. "I take French in school."

"Then we should understand each other very well," he stated, as he sat back down.

Joey was glad that Jean-Pierre wanted to eat in the pub instead of the pandemonium of the cafeteria. She was looking forward to getting to know him better. "Are you ready for the big race?" Joey asked as she glanced at the menu. "You don't seem to be the least bit nervous."

"I am never nervous," Jean-Pierre stated. "I am that good at racing."

"Oh. Okay," Joey said in surprise at his bold statement. "I'm bringing all my friends to help cheer you on. I'll introduce you—you'd like them."

"I don't care about your friends," he said rudely, closing his menu. "I'm just happy to have a pretty girl cheering me on. You see, my girlfriend broke up with me at the beginning of the season. Without a pretty girl it is not the same."

Great, Joey thought. If possible, Jean-Pierre was turning out to be a bigger jerk than Stinky. So her sole purpose was to stand there and look pretty for Jean-Pierre, no doubt to impress his teammates—or himself.

Well, she figured, if she was being used for a slope ornament, she might as well suffer through it and get a free lunch. She had to go to the race to meet her friends, plus, she didn't want to give up her fantasy yet—the fantasy of two men vying for her attention. She had to admit that it was fun to be the envy of both Jen and Dawson. She'd play out the dream for a little bit longer.

Too bad the reality wasn't nearly as exciting.

Dawson unstrapped his foot from his board and helped Jen plant her skis in the snow. The two of them walked over to the sidelines at the bottom of the racecourse, keeping an eye out for Pacey and Joey.

He had a great time skiing with Jen today. She seemed to put her troubles aside, determined to have fun. Dawson admired that; many people wouldn't be able to handle themselves as well as Jen did.

And the more he thought about how he set her up as a pawn in a game of "Make Joey Jealous," the angrier he became with himself. All he did was make a show of asking her to ski with him, and then knock her down in the snow in front of Joey. But that was enough to make him feel bad, and it was going to stop there.

Dawson had been searching his mind all day for a Joey Plan B, but he was coming up blank. He was even considering dropping the whole thing, making what was left of the weekend a Joey-free zone. But it was hard to do that when he was sitting through this race just for her. What he really wanted was to get back on the slopes.

Jen pointed out Pacey, holding hands with Kyra at the end of a line of spectators. They walked up behind the happy couple and Dawson poked Pacey in the back. "What's up?" Dawson asked.

Pacey turned around, beaming. "Dawson, my man. Jen, my woman. How was your morning?"

"Excellent," Jen said, while Dawson agreed. Dawson couldn't get over Pacey's transformation. Just a week ago, Pacey was a grumbling, insecure mass of neuroses. Now, he was smiling, self-confident, and without a care in the world—except for the lovely girl by his side.

Dawson saw Joey walk over. She looked a little surly at first, but her expression changed when she noticed her friends. "Hi guys," she called. "This is my first ski-race ever. It's pretty exciting. I hope Jean-Pierre and his team sweep."

"Ladies and gentlemen," a voice boomed over the loudspeaker just then. "We welcome you to Steep Mountain's annual invitational slalom. Thank you for coming. Enjoy the race, and come back tomorrow for our amateur competition!"

"Which guy are we supposed to be rooting for?" Dawson asked Joey, hoping that the race wouldn't last too long.

"Only Montreal's best young skier, Jean-Pierre Mouly," Joey said smugly.

Dawson scoffed. "Oh, did he tell you that? I'll bet there are many French-Canadians who beg to differ."

Joey's expression turned cross. "It's the truth," she said. "He's won more races than anyone in his league."

"Okay," Dawson said, putting his hands up, jealousy eating at his gut. Joey barely knew this guy and she was acting like he was king of the world. "I mean, it's not like he's a tri-athlete or anything.

How hard can speeding down a hill be, anyway? Gravity does most of the work."

Joey turned on Dawson, her expression sour. "Oh yeah? It's easy to knock something when you can't do it."

Dawson laughed. "I happen to be an excellent skier. And I bet you that guy can't ride a board for nothing."

Before Joey could respond, the crowd hushed. The races were about to begin.

"Ladies and gentlemen, skiing for the University of Montreal, Jean-Pierre Mouly."

"Oh, he's first," Joey said. She gave Dawson a half-sneer as she cheered. "Go Jean-Pierre! Go!"

Whoosh! Jean-Pierre was out of the gate, looking lean and sleek as he crouched, picking up speed by pushing off his skis. He effortlessly rounded the first flag, then carved around to the second, then on and on.

"Wow," Jen said. "He has so much control for someone going so fast. I'll bet his muscular movements have to be so precise, so as not to throw off his balance or lose a smidgen of a second."

Dawson shot Jen a withering look. She was just making it worse.

"Go! *Allez!*" Joey continued cheering.

Jean-Pierre crossed the line and, Dawson had to admit, racked up an impressive time. But Dawson hung around to see how he compared to the others.

As the competition went on, skiers from several U.S. and Canadian teams raced. Jean-Pierre placed fifth in the end, which, considering the number of participants, was very good, Dawson realized. But he wasn't first and "best" after all.

"Looks like 'the best skier in Montreal' isn't so hot when it comes to real competition," Dawson observed loudly.

"Typical thing for a couch potato who lives his whole life watching movies to say," Joey retorted, just before she raced over to congratulate Jean-Pierre.

Dawson reeled from her insult. Couch potato? Who was Joey calling a couch potato?

A voice boomed from the loudspeaker once again. "Thank you, ladies and gentlemen, for joining us. Please join us tomorrow for the amateur competition. All those interested in signing up, pick up a qualifying questionnaire at the finish line."

Inadvertently, Dawson stumbled upon his Plan B. He fumed inside. The amateur competition was the perfect way to get Joey's attention, and to show her that he was no couch potato. And just so he wouldn't be compared to Jean-Pierre, Dawson would enter the snowboard slalom.

"Where do I get this qualifying thing?" Dawson asked Pacey.

"You're going to enter?" Pacey asked, releasing Kyra's hand for the first time during the race. "Have you ever raced before? It's harder than it looks. The hill suddenly seems a whole lot steeper when you have to go in a straight line to hit those flags."

"I'm entering," Dawson said, his mouth a grim, determined line. "I know I can do it."

"Hey, Dawson," Jen said, gently patting him on the shoulder. "This macho routine doesn't become you at all. Just forget about it. Why bite off more than you can chew?"

Dawson shook his head in bewilderment. He couldn't believe that his own friends didn't believe in him. "Now you think I'm a wimp, too? I can't believe you guys!"

"No one's calling you a wimp, Dawson," Jen said firmly. "I just think it's silly for you to enter a competition because Joey called you a name, that's all. You don't have to prove anything to anyone."

"Yeah," Pacey agreed. "Who cares anyway. Ski team. Big deal. These guys probably don't know anything about filmmaking."

Dawson's friends weren't swaying him one bit. "I'm not a couch potato," he said angrily. "And I'm going to enter that race." Shooting Jen and Pacey a scornful look, he added, "I just hope that you're more supportive tomorrow."

He stalked off to the finish line, even more determined to set Joey—and his friends—straight.

Chapter 15

Pacey sat on the bench next to the entrance of the Treehouse, a charming little spot that Jen had suggested to him as a good date place. He wanted to take Kyra somewhere nice and memorable for their last night together.

Their last night! Pacey couldn't believe it. They had just met, and now he had to go back to Capeside, home of the Witter Museum of Family War. Capeside, where girls treated him like he had some kind of incurable disease. Capeside, completely absent of all winter sports. Dullsville.

He hadn't felt this way since he and Andie first started to fall for each other. Kyra felt like his soulmate. She was someone around whom he could chuck his insecurities and really be himself; around her, Pacey felt attractive, intelligent, witty, and fun to be around. He liked the person he was around Kyra.

126

What was he going to do without her? Fortunately Steep Mountain was only a few hours from Capeside. They could get together on weekends. If he ever got his driving privileges back.

Driving privileges. Dad. Ugh. He didn't want to think about going home. He buried thoughts of home with images of the day they had shared together. Pacey had so much fun teaching her how to ride today. By the time they had gone to see the race, she was steadily improving. Pacey had joked that mankind would now be safer from her spiraling wipeouts.

He glanced at his watch. She'd be there soon. Pacey enjoyed sitting outside and waiting for his girl. The cool night air seemed to crystallize his thoughts. Everything seemed clear; anything seemed possible.

He stared at his reflection in the window of the restaurant. He was lucky that even the nicest restaurants in Vermont were pretty casual. It was hard to see if he looked okay in the frosty glass that nearly obscured a "Help Wanted" sign. He turned around when he heard footsteps approach.

His heart leaped when he saw Kyra. Rising from the wooden bench, he caught Kyra in his arms and gave her a jubilant kiss.

"This is one of the nicest restaurants in town," Kyra said. "You don't have to do this—"

"Only the best for you," Pacey said, pulling a small white rose from his jacket pocket and placing it in her hair. He opened the door, and gestured her inside. "After you, Mademoiselle," he said.

Kyra looked around the cozy restaurant in amazement. "I've never been here before," she said. "How did you know about it?"

"Grueling research," he lied.

Jen had certainly steered him right tonight; he owed her one. The Treehouse was a perfect name for the charming, romantic restaurant. Everywhere, limbs and trunks and twigs and bark surrounded them. Brown, gold, and orange leaves decorated the walls, and the rustic wooden tables displayed fresh winter flowers in the center. A fireplace warmed the small space from the corner, crackling peacefully in time to the classical music that played softly in the background.

The waiter led them to a table with large, high-backed oak chairs. Pacey regarded the polished wood floors, then accepted a menu made out of cork and homemade paper. "Geez," he noted, "I wonder how many trees they killed to build this place."

Kyra laughed so hard she nearly spit out a sip of water. She had a knack for making Pacey feel like the funniest guy in the world.

Tonight, he wanted to make sure they had a night to remember. If only he knew when he'd be able to see her again.

Suddenly, an image flooded in his mind from before—the frost-covered window. It triggered a terrific idea; the answer to all of his troubles. He had to do a little investigation first, but if his idea worked out, he would never be unhappy again.

Excitement bubbled up inside of him as he ordered his meal. Kyra would flip. But again, he had some legwork to do. It just had to work, but just in case, he'd sit on it for now.

Tomorrow, he'd give her the good news.

Joey slipped on the bathing suit that Jen had loaned her. She was looking forward to a nice, relaxing soak in the hot tub. She didn't have any dates tonight, which was more than fine with her. She needed a break from the battle of the egomaniacs anyway.

Living a fantasy and keeping up appearances was exhausting, she realized. Even though she was so turned off by Jean-Pierre at lunch, Dawson was acting like such a jerk that she decided to cheer him on like a Cowboys cheerleader.

She grabbed a towel and trotted down the stairs. When she opened the door to the hot tub room, she was disappointed to see that Dawson was already in it.

Part of her wanted to turn around and leave. But her stubborn streak told her to stay. If she wanted to sit in the hot tub, she should do just that.

Silently, she climbed up the short, wooden ladder and lowered herself into the steamy water.

"It feels great in here," Dawson said, obviously trying to make conversation. "This will be great for my muscles for the amateur race tomorrow. Bet you didn't know that I was participating."

Joey just grunted in response, wishing she had brought a magazine or something. She didn't want to make idle chatter; she just wanted to relax and soak her overworked, aching muscles.

"How did your last lesson go?" Dawson asked, not giving up.

"Fine," Joey answered curtly.

"Once you learn, you'll never forget. It's like riding a bicycle," he continued.

Joey grunted again, and the door opened, throwing a shaft of light and a draft their way. Jen walked in the room then shut the door behind her. "Ooooh! A pool party!" she joked.

Just what Joey wanted. A crowd. She threw her head back and shut her eyes, pretending she was all alone in a dark, hot room.

Jen lowered herself in the tub, immediately breaking Joey's illusion with a question. "No dates tonight?" Jen pointedly asked.

Joey opened her eyes and shook her head. "Jean-Pierre was too beat from the race, and Stinky had night shift at First Aid."

Jen nodded.

"I guess it's feast or famine," Dawson chided.

Joey ignored him. She was tired of talking. She closed her eyes again and wished everyone else away.

The trio sat in silence for a few minutes. It was getting hot in the tub, and Joey started to feel a little lightheaded, but she didn't want to move.

She had almost started to feel alone and far away, when Dawson spoke again. "So, who's going to be the lucky guy? Are you going to choose between the two or just dump them both tomorrow?"

Joey flipped her eyes open and glared at Dawson. What was his problem? "Last time I checked it was none of your business," she snapped.

"Sorry," Dawson said defensively. "You're right. If you want to use people, that's your own business. Far be it for me to remind you that they're also human beings. With feelings. Even if they are men."

Joey just stared at Dawson, then broke into uproarious laughter. The thought of either Stinky or Jean-Pierre as sensitive beings was hysterical.

Jen stood up and climbed out of the tub. "I'm not in the mood to listen to bickering." She wrapped a towel around herself. "Dawson, why don't you just chill out. Let Joey live her life. Stop trying to manipulate her back into your life."

Joey couldn't believe that Jen was coming to her defense, especially after she'd been acting so sulky and jealous. When Jen left the room, Joey decided to leave, too. She just wanted to relax, and staying in the tub with Dawson was a recipe for an argument festival.

As Joey stood, she felt Dawson's hand clamp on her wrist. "Wait," he said softly. "She's right. In my head, I had planned for this to be the weekend that you would come running back into my arms. I orchestrated little things so you'd get jealous. Then I signed up for this race tomorrow to get your attention, too. I guess I thought I could control your feelings. I can't; and I'm sorry I tried to."

Joey sat back down in the tub. For the first time the entire weekend, she felt like Dawson was being real. "Well," she said. "I have to admit. Some of it worked. I was a little . . . surprised about you and Jen getting so chummy all over again. And I'm kind of flattered that you'd sign up for a race just for me." She started laughing again. "Actually, I'm more amused by it than flattered."

It struck Joey that Dawson wasn't the only one who was playing games. Didn't she tolerate Jean-Pierre and Stinky simply to make Jen—and Dawson—jealous? She, too, was manipulating people.

Suddenly, the difference between Dawson and guys like Jean-Pierre and Stinky became clear. Dawson was so interested in Joey as a person. Jean-Pierre and Stinky couldn't care less about her interests and ideas. Joey started to giggle, feeling a little lightheaded from the steam.

Dawson shifted in the tub. "I should apologize to Jen. This is her cabin, and we drove her out of her own hot tub."

"Wait!" Joey said urgently. Suddenly, inexplicably, she wanted to kiss Dawson, for being himself, for not being like other guys.

She did. She slid over and placed her mouth on his. Dawson instantly responded, grabbing her and hugging her close.

Joey felt like she was in a heavenly dream, the rising steam around them like clouds. Kissing Dawson, right at that moment, felt like paradise.

But then a flash of cool air caught them as Jen threw open the door. "I guess you're done arguing—" she started.

Joey and Dawson pulled apart in surprise.

Jen's shocked expression shook Joey out of her reverie.

What in the world had she just done?

* * *

Jen closed the door, and walked numbly up to the master bedroom. She wondered why men were such philanderers. How could Dawson be kissing her one night, then Joey the next? Didn't any man care about women's feelings?

It wasn't that she was upset that Dawson and Joey were kissing. She was actually kind of happy about that; she knew it was what Dawson had been praying for all weekend.

But it brought back the problem of her two-timing father, the thing she had tried to forget about all day. Dawson's confusion seemed so human. It made her wonder—was her dad as confused?

But Dawson was a teenaged boy. Her father was middle-aged. By now, her dad should know what he wanted in life, and as much as the prospect of her parents divorcing pained her, she thought that if her parents found themselves in a situation they no longer wanted to be in, then they should just call it quits. Why force love's hand?

Good question. Half the time she didn't know what she wanted, either. One day, she wanted Dawson back. The next day, she couldn't care less. She realized it had nothing to do with Dawson, and everything to do with her.

Jen decided that when her parents returned from England, she'd talk to her dad, get the whole story, and try as hard as she could to be understanding.

There was a knock on her door. "Come in," she called, realizing it was probably Dawson.

She was right.

"I don't know what to say," Dawson said, sitting on the bed. "You were right. I used you to get to

Joey. But I didn't orchestrate kissing you in front of the fire. And I shouldn't have been kissing Joey just now . . ."

"Don't worry about it," Jen said, giving Dawson a hug. "Go for it—you and Joey belong together. I don't know if she'll ever come around, but you should try your best." She let out a breath, feeling as if a huge weight was being lifted off her chest. "And I'm sorry, too, if I gave you mixed signals. I'm just as confused as the next guy. But I want to stay good friends, okay?"

Dawson smiled, then returned Jen's hug. "That sounds great. I need a friend right now," he said.

"You should get back down there," Jen said, playfully slapping him on the shoulder. "After a kiss like that I hope you just didn't up and leave her in the tub."

Dawson nodded. "I did. But she looked so stricken after we kissed—like she didn't even realize it was me—that I figured she wanted me to leave her alone."

"Take my advice, Dawson," Jen said. "Let it go for a while. It happened. Let her sort out what she's going through. Tomorrow, I don't think she'll have any regrets about sending these Johnny-come-latelys away. Give her some time to realize who's been there all along."

Dawson nodded. "Thanks, friend."

Jen smiled. Right then and there she decided that the best feeling in the world was being a good friend.

Pacey sauntered into the cabin late, finding Dawson, Jen, and Joey lazily reading by the fire in the family room. What a night he'd had! He wanted to tell his friends all about it.

"Evening, folks," he said cheerfully as he stretched out on the rug and poked at the fire. "How was your night?"

The threesome seemed to exchange weird, amused looks. Dawson finally spoke. "It was okay. How was yours?"

"Fantastic," he said, all of the emotions of the evening bubbling up and coming back. "Jen, I owe you one. Great call on the Treehouse. She loved it!"

"Great," Jen said, with a yawn. "At your service anytime."

"Are you going to spend the day with Kyra tomorrow?" Joey remarked, looking up from her magazine.

Pacey nodded, throwing another log on the fire.

"Don't forget to come watch my race. Bring Kyra along. I'll need all the support I can get," Dawson said.

"You're really going to do that?" Pacey asked incredulously.

"Yeah," Dawson answered. "I'm committed now. I'm signed up and everything."

Joey shot Dawson an approving smile. "You can count on us all to be there cheering you on."

Dawson was probably on cloud nine because of Joey's encouragement. Pacey just hoped he wouldn't end up completely humiliated. But he didn't want to dwell on Dawson and his girl troubles right now; he had things of his own to sort out. The wheels in his head where turning . . .

"I'll bet it's going to be hard for you to say goodbye to Kyra tomorrow," Jen said fondly, cutting into Pacey's thoughts.

Pacey snapped out of his dreamworld. "Not really," he said.

"What?" Joey asked, closing her magazine. "You're crazy about her. It's written all over you."

Pacey nodded, holding up his hands. "I'm not sorry to say goodbye to her because I'm not going to be saying goodbye—that's the thing. I've been thinking about this all night, and I think I can make it work. I haven't even told her yet, but I will tomorrow. I just need to get a little more information—"

"Whoa!" Dawson said. "Wait a minute. You're not making any sense. What are you talking about?"

Pacey took in a deep breath. "Okay. From the beginning. Tonight, at that fabulous restaurant, I noticed a Help Wanted sign in the window. I talked to the manager briefly when Kyra went to the bathroom. It turns out they pay pretty well, and the tips are supposed to be amazing."

Pausing, and taking in all the shocked expressions on his friends' faces, Pacey went on. "So, I was thinking. Why does it have to be goodbye? Why can't it be hello? What if I was to move here? I'd get away from my family, who doesn't care about my existence anyway. And I'd be near Kyra. I want to check out the paper in the morning about getting a cheap apartment—"

"Hold on!" Dawson cut in again. "What about school? What about Screen Play? What about us?"

Pacey could see that Dawson was upset. Jen and Joey just seemed completely shocked. "I don't think Capeside High would be devastated without me.

Same goes for Screen Play. After a while, I could probably enroll in school here, anyway, and work at nights."

"And, by the time you make your rent money, that would leave you approximately zero time with Kyra," Joey added.

Pacey started to grow annoyed. Here he was sharing the happiest news of his life, and his friends didn't seem the least bit happy for him. "I can make it work," he said, determined. "It's worth it for me. A new life. The type of girl I always dreamed of being with."

"You're sixteen," Dawson said. "And you didn't answer my other questions. What about us?"

"I'll drive you home, pack up my stuff, and take a bus back here," Pacey responded. "Don't worry."

Dawson shook his head with impatience. "No, dude, I mean what about *us*? You don't have any friends in Steep Mountain. You're just going to leave your lifelong friends behind?"

Pacey was touched that Dawson would actually miss him. He was one of the few people in Capeside who would. "Hey, Dawson," Pacey said, standing and patting his buddy on the back. "It's only a couple of hours away. I'll visit. You'll visit. No big deal."

"What about Kyra?" Joey asked sharply. "She approves of this? And her father, too?"

"Kyra doesn't know yet," Pacey admitted. "But she will tomorrow. I'm going to work out all the details, then surprise her."

His three friends fell silent again, their expressions dumbfounded. Typical of them not to have any faith in him, Pacey thought. Why should they be different from anyone else?

They were just immature, afraid to leave the safe haven of their homes, happy or not. Pacey wasn't going to let himself fall into that trap. He was breaking out on his own, and he couldn't wait.

Chapter 16

"**S**tinky!" Joey said in surprise early the next afternoon. She and the gang had gotten to the mountain early to ski and then catch the races. After lunch, they were going to return to the cabin and pack up and go.

Not a minute too soon, Joey thought. She wanted to go back home and resume her life as regular old Joey Potter. It was hard work being a man-magnet. "What are you doing here?" she asked.

"I have the morning off because I worked late last night," he said, smiling and showing his dreamy dimples. "So, where would I rather be but with you on your last day!" He leaned in and gave her a peck on the cheek.

Great, Joey thought. Just when she wanted to have a peaceful day on her own. Men—they were such pests.

"Oh! *Bonjour!*" she heard Jen say loudly. Joey looked down the spectator line at her, and caught Jen's conspiratorial glance as she chatted with Jean-Pierre, turning him so his back was to Joey.

Another pest for the party, Joey thought. She was grateful that Jen was helping her out and that, because of her efforts, Jean-Pierre hadn't seen her yet. Joey wanted to creep away—from both guys—somehow.

But right at that moment, Stinky clutched Joey's hand and brought it to his heart. "I wanted to thank you for the glowing evaluation, and I also wanted you to know that I am going to miss you so much," he declared. "I won't rest until you come back to Steep Mountain."

How dramatic, Joey thought, trying her best not to laugh. He didn't even take the time to stop talking about himself long enough to get to know her. How could he possibly miss her?

"That's so sweet," Joey said, wondering how she was going to get her hand out of his grip. Jen was stalling and still talking to Jean-Pierre, but he'd be smack next to them in a split second. "Uh—I have an itch," she said, pulling her hand away.

"Then I'll scratch it," Stinky said, pulling Joey close.

"*Qu'est que c'est?*" she suddenly heard behind her. "What is going on? Joey? Who is this octopus with his tentacles around you?"

Stinky dropped his arms from Joey's waist. "Who the hell are you?" he challenged, walking up to Jean-Pierre and staring him in the face.

"I am her boyfriend. She is my girl," Jean-Pierre said.

"What are you talking about? I've been seeing her since Saturday," Stinky defended.

Both guys turned to Joey, who just shrugged her shoulders. She didn't consider either of them her boyfriend—not Jean-Pierre, who thought a girl's purpose was to cheer for him, and not Stinky, who thought it was a girl's joy to listen to him ad nauseum.

"Ah!" Jean-Pierre said, throwing his hands up in the air. "I should have known! Trampy American girls!"

"No one two-times me!" Stinky added.

Then Joey started to laugh at their hilarious antics. She was pleased she was the one to give them each a small taste of reality.

Jean-Pierre and Stinky stared at Joey, bewildered as she laughed and laughed, so hard she thought she'd never stop.

"Well, dude, I'm not going to hang around here anymore. Can I buy you a beer at the pub?" Stinky offered.

Jean-Pierre shrugged. "Sure. Why not. Maybe there will be some cute chicks there."

Without another word, Joey's two weekend warriors strolled off.

"Wow," Jen said, a look of amazement on her face. "That was . . . hmmm . . . I'm not sure how to describe that scene," she said, laughing along with Joey.

Joey sucked in a deep breath. "How about surreal? Absurd? Outrageous?"

Jen nodded. "Yes, exactly," she agreed. "I'd also add grotesque and ridiculous."

The girls turned their attentions to the race, when the announcement starting the race came over the loudspeaker. The first race was to be the amateur snowboard slalom—Dawson's race.

"Wish me luck," Dawson said, sliding by them to get on the chairlift up to the starting gate. "I'm third."

"Good luck," Jen said.

"Yeah," Joey added. "And Dawson . . . I'm proud of you. You're not a couch potato."

A huge smile lit up Dawson's face. "Thanks, Joey," he called.

The first competitor flew down the mountain, but Joey didn't pay much attention to him. She was wondering where Pacey and Kyra were. Pacey had said they'd be there in time for the race, but there was no sign of them. Joey figured Pacey was probably delivering his bit of news to Kyra right at that very moment.

Pacey searched the cafeteria for a table, and he finally spotted an empty one. Hustling over, he placed the tray with two steaming hot chocolates down, then pulled out a chair for Kyra. He sat down himself, across from her.

"What's your big news?" Kyra asked excitedly. "Tell me before I burst from curiosity!"

Pacey drew in a deep breath. He thought he'd burst, too, from excitement. "Okay," he said. "I wanted to let you know that I'm not saying goodbye to you today."

Kyra's face lit up. "You mean you're staying an extra day? Awesome! But I do have to go back to school tomorrow . . ."

Pacey shook his head. "No, that's not it. I'm not going to say goodbye because I'm not going anywhere. I'm moving here, to Steep Mountain."

Kyra's expression changed from excitement to confusion. "What? Your family's moving here all of a sudden? I don't understand—"

"I'm sparing you my family," Pacey cut in, grabbing Kyra's hand. "It's just me. I'm moving here. I'm driving my friends back to Capeside, packing up my stuff, and hopping on the next bus out."

Now Kyra looked dumbfounded. "What? Why would you do that?"

Pacey was taken aback. This was certainly not the reaction he was expecting. "For us," he said, nerves making his stomach flutter. "Don't you think it's a good idea?"

Now Kyra looked like a deer caught in headlights. "Well, that's very touching, but . . ."

"But what?" Pacey asked, hurt. He thought she would be leaping for joy, kissing him all over. What was with her?

"Well, what about school, for example? And where are you going to live? Dad would never let you stay with us. And . . . and . . ."

So she was concerned about the logistics. Pacey expected that. "It's all taken care of. I'm going to apply for a job at the Treehouse, to work nights, and I checked the paper and there are plenty of daytime jobs I could take. There's an opening at the convenience store, for one. And I'll work both jobs until I can cover my first couple of months' rent, and then I'll re-enroll in school, if it's really important to you. But don't expect me to graduate with honors or anything. I'm not much of a student."

Kyra shook her head, taking her hand out of Pacey's. "This is the most ridiculous thing I've ever heard. What about your family? What about your friends? You're going to leave all of them . . . just to be near me?"

"My family is like something from a psychologist's textbook about dysfunction," Pacey answered. "I won't be missing them, and I doubt very much they'll be missing me. My friends, I'll miss, but hey—it's only a couple of hours' drive."

"But you're too young—we're too young. You barely know me," Kyra said, flustered. "I'm sorry, but I don't think this is a good idea at all, Pacey."

Kyra might as well drive a knife into my heart, Pacey thought, and turn it several times. He couldn't believe that she didn't want him around, either. What is it about me that makes everyone who gets to know me want to run far away? he wondered. "So, didn't these past few days mean anything to you?" he asked sadly. "Anything at all? Or does this happen to you all the time?"

Kyra softened, taking Pacey's hand back. "Look, Pacey. I've loved being with you. You're the most amazing guy I've ever met," she said tenderly. "But I don't want to be responsible for you throwing your life away. After quitting school and working twenty-four hours a day, you're going to see opportunities pass you by. And you'll become bitter." She shook her head. "I don't want you to end up unhappy because of me."

"But I won't be unhappy," Pacey insisted. "If I'm near you, I'll be happy. You're all I need."

"Don't, Pacey," Kyra said firmly, rising from the table. "Go back to Capeside, where you belong. I don't want you to come here."

"Wait! Don't go!" Pacey called after her as she walked away. His dreams had turned out to be a total nightmare. What had gotten into Kyra? Why did she just get up and leave like that?"

Pacey sat back down and put his head in his hands. He was devastated. Just a few minutes ago, he saw a whole new life mapped out before him. Now it was all in pieces.

For a few wonderful days, Pacey finally felt like a winner. He felt like he was attractive—someone a girl liked to be around. Someone fun and clever and desirable.

But his inner-loser must have shown through, and Kyra saw it, clear as day. She didn't want to spend any more time with a loser, Pacey thought, and who could blame her.

And now he was all alone. Alone in the cafeteria with two cold hot chocolates and a broken heart.

Chapter 17

"**Y**ou're just in time to see Dawson's race," Jen said as Pacey slunk up to join her and Joey. "You almost missed it."

"Yeah, well, I'm here," Pacey muttered.

Jen could tell something was wrong. This was not the same Pacey who had been beaming with happiness and walking on air the whole weekend.

"Where's Kyra?" Joey asked, not even noticing Pacey's glum mood.

"I don't know," Pacey answered.

"What? You've been surgically attached to her for the past couple of days. How could you not know where she is?" Joey asked.

"Well, like an unsightly mole, I've been surgically removed. She doesn't want me to move here," he answered sadly.

Jen felt badly for Pacey, but she had seen it coming. Jen could tell Joey felt sorry for him, too. Here was a perfect opportunity for Joey to tell him what a dumb idea it was in the first place, but like Jen, she didn't say a word. His whole plan had been ridiculous, and in the blinding glare of infatuation he couldn't see that.

"Dawson's about to go," Joey said, pointing at the starting gate.

Jen turned her attention to the top of the hill. Dawson was ready and waiting. The gun fired. He was off.

Dawson got a good jump on the hill, and he cleared the first flag a little wide, but close enough for an amateur. He crouched and picked up speed to clear the next flag, then the next and the next, getting better every time.

"Go, Dawson!" Joey cheered.

"He's going way too fast!" Pacey said, alarmed. "Soon he won't have any control!"

Dawson zoomed, still trying to clear every flag. He blew past one, then hit the next, then rode flat over the next.

"See! He's in trouble!" Pacey warned. "I can't look."

The next flag tripped Dawson up, sending him spiraling, head over feet, down the rest of the mountain.

Jen drew in a breath and covered her mouth. Dawson kept tumbling, bouncing down the mountain.

"He has no idea what he's doing," Pacey groused, with an accusing look at Joey. "If you hadn't called him a couch potato, he wouldn't be up there,"

Pacey said. "You women—" he shook his head pityingly, "changing your feelings at the drop of a hat. You're all the same!"

Joey glared at him. "Remember that size twelve ski boot?" Joey asked Pacey. "Well you can insert it now."

"Stop it! Dawson's hurt," Jen said, as she saw him come to a stop, flat on his back at the bottom of the mountain.

Jen, Joey, and Pacey rushed over, following the first-aid team.

"Dawson!" Joey called, reaching his side and crouching down. "Are you okay?"

Jen peered over Joey's shoulder. Thankfully, Dawson was breathing, and he was conscious.

"Am I still alive?" Dawson croaked, sounding like he was only half-joking. He tried to sit up.

"Don't move yet, son," a paramedic said. "Catch your breath. You had your wind knocked out of you."

Jen watched as Dawson's short, quick breaths turned longer, slower, and deeper. Looking over her shoulder, she could see that a crowd was forming.

"Okay," the paramedic said. "I want you to slowly sit up."

Dawson cautiously lifted his torso. He threw out one hand to balance, then howled in pain when he placed his other hand down. "Ow!"

"What hurts?" the paramedic asked.

"My wrist," Dawson answered.

"Okay, we'll help you up," the other paramedic said. "We don't want you to place any weight on your wrist."

Gradually, Dawson stood up. Everything else seemed fine. He didn't hit his head too hard, and he didn't seem to have any broken limbs.

"Come on over to First Aid and we'll take a look at that wrist," the paramedic said.

The gang followed the first-aid team down to the lodge. Dawson didn't say a word the whole way. Jen figured it was an embarrassed silence.

Jen, Joey, and Pacey had to stay in the waiting room while a doctor checked Dawson out. Jen glanced at her watch. They had to get going soon if they wanted to be home by sundown.

"The crazy things we men do for love," Pacey said longingly.

Joey buried her face in a magazine, Jen noticed, ignoring Pacey's comment, while Dawson emerged from the doctor's office.

He wore a brace on his wrist. "Sprained," Dawson explained when he came out. "So," he went on. "Who wants to be the first to tell me what a fool I made out of myself?"

"You're not alone, buddy," Pacey said, standing up and patting Dawson on the back.

Jen and Joey didn't say a word.

Dawson felt like a first-class heel when they got back to the cabin. It wasn't going to be fun explaining the brace to his parents, though after much concern and a lecture about safety on the slopes he hoped it wouldn't be so bad.

He packed up his things and was actually looking forward to getting home. The weekend didn't turn out as he had planned.

He heard a tap on his door. "Yeah," he said.

Joey stepped into his room and sat in the wooden rocker in the corner. "That was dumb what you did, entering that race if you weren't prepared," she said. "And I want you to know that you didn't have to do it. You didn't have to go out of your way to impress me. The kiss last night was impressive enough."

Dawson lifted his bag off the bed with his good hand, and nearly dropped it on the floor with Joey's comment. They had pretty much avoided each other since the incident in the hot tub the previous night. He was glad she brought it up and even happier that she found it "impressive."

"Really?" Dawson asked incredulously.

"Yeah," Joey said, tucking a strand of chestnut hair behind her ear. "I miss those kisses," she went on. "And playing around with those jerks made me realize what a great guy you are."

Dawson broke out into a huge grin. "You mean—"

Joey shook her head. "No. I still don't want to get back together. But I want you to know that I'm not a total ice queen. There are feelings there—a lot of feelings. But I still need to be on my own."

Dawson's face fell. "Okay," he whispered.

"Please save yourself the trouble of trying so hard, Dawson, before you require a longer hospital stay. Let's work on the friendship, instead," she said gently. "Let's make it stronger."

"Okay," Dawson responded, though he knew deep inside that he really wasn't okay. He still wanted Joey back more than ever, and he didn't know if his desire for her would ever go away.

But he wanted to be close to her. Being her friend was better than nothing.

"I have to go back and finish packing," Joey said.

"Sure," Dawson said. When the door closed behind her, he sat on his bed. He had gotten his hopes up once again, just to have them stomped on. And he was tired of disappointment, tired of pining.

As he walked toward the door, he stopped at the mirror. "Leery, you have got to toughen up," he said. Right then and there he decided that he needed to take a break from being young and in love.

He just wished it was easier done than said.

When Jen came downstairs, ready to load up the car, the phone rang. She wondered who would be calling. It was probably a wrong number, she mused, as she picked up the phone.

"Jennifer?" she heard a familiar voice intone. Her heart sank. It was her mother. Poor, unknowing, Mom.

"Hey, Mom," she answered. "Where are you?"

"We're still in London. I don't have a lot of time to talk. I was just calling to see if everything was okay at the cabin and to see if you had a good time."

No, everything was not okay, Jen wanted to tell her. Dad's cheating on you right in your own cabin.

But she restrained herself. "Everything was fine. We had fun."

"You picked the perfect weekend, you know," her

mother continued. "Any other weekend the Martins might have been there."

Jen caught her breath and stopped. "The who?" she asked, not sure what her mother was talking about.

"The Martins—that newlywed couple who are renting it for a half-share this season. Didn't we tell you about them?"

Jen gasped. She felt a heavy weight drop from her shoulders. A newlywed couple? "You mean—that's their stuff here—" she asked, not believing her luck at the mix-up.

"Yes," her mother said. "Except they shouldn't have too much there—there's no furniture or anything—or pets—is there?"

"No, no," Jen said, relieved. "Everything is just as it was." And she really meant that. Her family—and her parents' marriage—wasn't in crisis after all.

"Okay sweetheart," Jen's mother went on. "We'll call you up at Grams' when we get home. Have a safe trip back to Capeside."

"Bye, Mom," Jen said. She hung up, a huge grin on her face.

"What's going on?" Dawson asked, as he and Pacey dragged their bags down the stairs.

Jen ran to Dawson and told him everything. Dawson hugged her, and she wished that his own parents' problems were just a misunderstanding. But she knew better, and she admired how Dawson could share her relief despite his own situation.

"Let's load up," Jen announced as Joey came down the stairs. "Then I'll lock up."

She led the gang out the door, but stopped short

when she noticed a pink envelope on the floor. It looked like someone had slid it under the door.

Bending to examine it, Jen could see the name "Pacey" written on it in neat, loopy handwriting.

"What's that?" Pacey asked, coming up behind her and peering over her shoulder.

"It's for you," Jen said, handing it over. She had a pretty good idea who it was from.

Chapter 18

Dear Pacey,

I'm so sorry about the way we left off, and I
did want to say goodbye, though I hope it's not
goodbye forever.

I don't want you to misunderstand me; I do
want to be around you, but moving here isn't
going to solve your problems at home. Like I said,
when you grow tired and homesick and lonely, I
don't want to feel responsible for taking you away
from your home and friends.

I'm sorry I left you at the cafeteria like that.
But at that point, I felt that "tough love" was the
best tactic. Hopefully you've had time to think
now and you realize what I was trying to say.

The truth is that I do want to be around you
as much as possible, that's why I'm including my
address and phone number. Please feel free to call

and come out to visit anytime. I hope you will call, and give me your address, too, so I can call, write, and perhaps spend some time in pretty Capeside.

Please know, Pacey, that these past couple of days have been the best of my life. I've had such a great time getting to know you, and I think you are an amazing guy. I want so much to see you again. I'm crazy about you. But if you're upset about this afternoon, I'll understand, though I'll be quite heartbroken.

Please keep in touch. Steep Mountain is going to be cold and lonely without your warm heart and smile.

Love,
Kyra

Pacey finished the letter and stuffed it into his pocket. "Let's go! Are we all ready?" he asked.

"I just need to check the house," Jen said. She ran upstairs and down, checking all the rooms, switching off the lights, and taking out the garbage.

So, Kyra did feel the same way about him, Pacey thought, intoxicated by the realization. Now that he saw it in writing, without his emotions clouding every word, twisting and turning the meaning, he realized that maybe it was a little forward and scary and crazy for him to consider moving here this soon.

Maybe someday, if things worked out, they could be together. But now, he had to concentrate on first things first, and his first priority now was saying a proper goodbye to Kyra.

"Come on! Hurry!" Pacey bellowed. "We have a pitstop to make. Everybody in the car!"

"All right already. Sheesh!" Joey said, scampering past him, out the door. She dropped her bag in the trunk and opened the back door. "Who would have known that frilly little pink envelope could turn someone from Mopey Dick to Jaws in a split second?"

Pacey was nearly jumping out of his skin. Finally, Dawson emerged from the cabin, then joined Joey in the backseat.

"Okay, I'm coming," Jen shouted, as she ran out of the cabin, closing and locking the door behind her.

"Finally!" Pacey said as he slammed into the driver's seat, and Jen took shotgun next to him. He revved up the motor and backed out of the long, narrow driveway.

"Easy, buddy," Dawson cautioned from the backseat. "Don't forget whose car, and whose ass, is on the line here."

"Believe me," Pacey said, angling the car onto the dirt road. "I want to get where we're going first in one piece." He put the car in gear. "After that, I don't care what happens."

"Great," Joey said. "Just great."

Pacey was glad that he had driven Kyra home the other night. Now he knew exactly where to go. He followed the dirt road out onto Main Street, hung a left, passed Paolo's Pizza and the Bowling Barn.

Within minutes, they pulled up to the small gray barn. Pacey shifted into park and hopped out of the car, not even turning the engine off.

"Kyra!" he called. "Kyra!" He ran up the front porch and knocked on the door wildly. "Kyra! Please be home!"

After a few seconds, the door opened, and Pacey saw a familiar pair of green eyes peek out at him.

"Hi," she said uncertainly.

"Hi," Pacey answered, a warmth of feelings rushing over him. "I got your letter. I came to say a proper goodbye. But not forever," he quickly added.

Kyra smiled and stepped out of her house, while Pacey pulled a piece of paper and pen from his pocket. "Here's my address and phone number," he said as he scribbled wildly. "I hope you make good use of it."

"I'll commit it to memory," she answered.

"Okay, then," Pacey said, trying to make the moment last, even if it was painful and awkward, and he had three people waiting in the car. But he didn't want to leave those beautiful green eyes behind. He knew he'd never forget those laughing eyes and her dazzling smile. The auburn color of her hair would never fade in his memory.

"Goodbye," Pacey said, then grabbed Kyra, pulling her toward him. He kissed her, pouring out all of his affection, drinking in her sweetness so he could savor it the whole ride home.

After a moment, they pulled apart. "I'll call you the second I'm back in Capeside," Pacey said.

"I'll miss you," Kyra whispered.

Pacey waved and turned to make the long walk to the car, where his friends were waiting impatiently. He had to go when he saw the trickle of a tear in Kyra's eye, lest his own eyes well up.

He opened the car door and slid into the driver's seat. Suddenly, he heard a pair of hands clapping, then another two, then another.

"Well done, my friend," Dawson said.

"That was beautiful," Jen added.

"*Très romantique*," Joey agreed. "She's a lucky girl."

"You really think so?" Pacey asked, as he pulled out of Kyra's driveway, trying not to watch her as she grew smaller and smaller in his rearview mirror.

"Yes," Joey answered. "Very lucky."

Epilogue

"**P**ick up, Joey!" Bessie called. "I know we barely have any customers but you still have to work."

Joey got up from the table where she lingered with Dawson, Jen, and Pacey, and moved to the food window to pick up her order. There was just one other table of people in the Ice House that night, and it had been that slow ever since they returned from Vermont a few days before.

As Joey balanced her tray and walked it over to the waiting table, she reflected on the time they had the past weekend. In Steep Mountain, she was glamorous and sought-after, the object of three men's desires. Back in Capeside, she was just a hash wench, slaving away at a two-bit restaurant where even Dawson didn't take much notice of her anymore. But she was okay with that; their friendship was finally back on track because of it. For the last few days there hadn't been any jealous glares or hurt feelings. Just easy, comfortable companionship.

She dropped off her tray, asked the customers if they would like anything else, then proceeded back to the table where her friends sat. "Being back in reality stinks," she said, sighing.

"Tell me about it," Pacey agreed, taking a sip of soda.

"At least you have something to look forward to," Jen said, picking up a French fry. "Aren't you going out to Steep Mountain next weekend?"

Pacey nodded. "Kyra's dad arranged for me to stay with their neighbors."

Joey raised her eyebrows in surprise. "Wow! That's awfully nice of them. Those poor people have no idea what they're in for."

Pacey went on, "Yeah, it is really nice of them, and I plan to be the best guest possible so I'll be invited back."

Joey couldn't believe it. Another insult, ignored by Pacey. He was still like an alien from outer space, still under the love spell Kyra had cast on him the weekend before.

"I think that's great, Pacey," Jen said. "My life needs that kind of excitement right now. Sitting home with Grams every night and reading just doesn't cut it."

"I hear you," Joey said. Waitressing, school, and babysitting Alexander certainly was no barrel of laughs. Not to mention the sorry excuse for winter weather they continued to get. Still wet and cold, not cozy and snowy like in Vermont.

"Well," Dawson said. "Since our lives are so dull,

why don't we liven them up vicariously," he suggested.

"How?" Joey asked. This ought to be a good one, she thought.

"Through a good, old-fashioned movie night!" he answered.

"Somehow I knew you were going to say that," Joey responded. "But, I guess I have nothing better to do. Count me in."

"Me, too," Jen said.

Dawson looked to Pacey. "Nah," Pacey said. "I'm just going to go home and write Kyra a letter."

"Suit yourself," Dawson said. Turning to Joey he asked, "When do you get off?"

"Whenever those snails over there decide to finish," she answered. "But you guys go on ahead. Get everything set. I'll meet you at your house."

"Okay," Dawson said. They paid the bill, and Joey brought them their change. As her friends exited, she glared at the people at the other table. Why did some people eat so slowly?

She decided to kill the time by taking a rag and wiping up some tables. Someone tapped her on the shoulder. She whirled around—it was only her sister.

"I'll take it from here, kiddo," Bessie said. "Go on. Get out. There's not much to do here."

"Thanks," Joey said. Bessie could be so cool sometimes, and this was one of those times. She had been in such a good mood lately—giving her the weekend off, letting her hang with her friends in the restaurant. But for all the benefits it had on her social life, Joey still wished that business would pick up, for the sake of Bessie and Alexander.

Joey untied her apron and pulled on her winter jacket. Zipping it up, she opened the door.

Stepping out into the night, she couldn't believe what she saw. Big, puffy, white flakes of snow gently fell out of the night sky. It was beautiful; it was a miracle.

Joey stood at the door, taking in the peaceful, beautiful moment, breathing in the snowy night air.

It was the perfect moment.

Until she was smacked in the side of the head with a wet snowball.

"Ambush!" Dawson cried, and before she knew it, Joey was attacked from all sides.

She ran away, laughing, excited about what Capeside's first real winter night of the year might bring.

About the Creator/Executive Producer

Born in New Bern, North Carolina, Kevin Williamson studied theater and film at East Carolina University before moving to New York to pursue an acting career. He relocated to Los Angeles and took a job as an assistant to a music video director. Eventually deciding to explore his gift for storytelling, Williamson took an extension course in screenwriting at UCLA (University of California, Los Angeles).

Kevin Williamson has experienced incredible success in the film medium. His first feature film was *Scream*, directed by Wes Craven and starring Drew Barrymore, Courteney Cox, and Neve Campbell. He has also written other feature films including the psychological thriller *I Know What You Did Last Summer*, based on the Lois Duncan novel, and directed by Jim Gillespie. His first foray into television, *Dawson's Creek*™, has already received high praise from television critics for its honest portrayal of teen life.

K. S. Rodriguez is the author of *Dawson's Creek: Long Hot Summer, Dawson's Creek: The Official Scrapbook,* and a dozen other books for young readers. She lives in Manhattan with her husband, Ronnie.

Read more about Joey, Dawson, Pacey,
and Jen in these four new, original
Dawson's Creek™ stories.

Long Hot Summer

Calm Before the Storm

Shifting Into Overdrive

Major Meltdown

And don't miss:

DAWSON'S CREEK
The Official Postcard Book

DAWSON'S CREEK
The Official Scrapbook

Available now from Pocket Books

Visit Pocket Books on the World Wide Web
http://www.SimonSays.com

Visit the Sony website at
http://www.dawsonscreek.com

2041-01

BUFFY

THE VAMPIRE

SLAYER™

As long as there have been vampires, there has been the Slayer.
One girl in all the world, to find them where they gather and
to stop the spread of their evil and the swell of their numbers

Child of the Hunt
By Christopher Golden and Nancy Holder

Return to Chaos
By Craig Shaw Gardner

The Watcher's Guide
(The Totally Pointy Guide for the Ultimate Fan!)
By Christopher Golden and Nancy Holder

Based on the hit TV series created by Joss Whedon

Published by Pocket Books

POCKET
BOOKS